CENTRAL
PRESBYTERIAN
(GOUGAR)

SECRET VOW

SECRET  VOW

Kathy Cecala

A DUTTON BOOK

DUTTON
Published by the Penguin Group
Penguin Books USA Inc., 375 Hudson Street,
New York, New York 10014, U.S.A.
Penguin Books Ltd, 27 Wrights Lane, London W8 5TZ, England
Penguin Books Australia Ltd, Ringwood, Victoria, Australia
Penguin Books Canada Ltd, 10 Alcorn Avenue,
Toronto, Ontario, Canada M4V 3B2
Penguin Books (N.Z.) Ltd, 182–190 Wairau Road,
Auckland 10, New Zealand

Penguin Books Ltd, Registered Offices:
Harmondsworth, Middlesex, England

First published by Dutton, an imprint of Dutton Signet,
a division of Penguin Books USA Inc.
Distributed in Canada by McClelland & Stewart Inc.

First Printing, May, 1997
10   9   8   7   6   5   4   3   2   1

Copyright © Kathleen Cecala, 1997
All rights reserved

   REGISTERED TRADEMARK—MARCA REGISTRADA

LIBRARY OF CONGRESS CATALOGING-IN-PUBLICATION DATA:

Printed in the United States of America
Set in Goudy
Designed by Eve L. Kirch

PUBLISHER'S NOTE

This book is printed on acid-free paper. ∞

To Frank and Frankie

1

Late Spring, 1965

ROSE Connolly placed the last tray of seedlings into her flatbed truck, then glanced back at her greenhouses: Locked, empty, they glowed eerily against the predawn sky. May, she knew, was no sensible time for a retail gardener to shut down, but she was grateful, at least, for two weekends of brisk sales, a profitable Easter. She'd sold all of her Madonna lilies, dozens of potted tulips, most of her azaleas and her rarest Japanese maple. She filled her old truck with her frailest plants, those still in need of her care: herbs mostly—her specialty—but also clumps of tender perennials, and all those seedlings, vegetables and flowers started in January and February, nurtured through the tail end of a long, bleak Connecticut winter.

She dispensed the rest of her plants swiftly, secretly, under the cover of night, leaving pots of coveted trees and bushes and tropical plants on neighbors' porches. She placed two of her showiest rhododendrons on the steps of the church, St. Cyril's, then hurried away before anyone spotted her. But she couldn't resist running back with a hastily scrawled note: *Part shade, water daily. No fert. til next spring.*

She was up all night, delivering her orphans, then working out behind her own house, with flashlight and lantern and bare hands, prying out of the still-cold, inky soil her own prized perennials, tender shoots of peonies and phlox and foxglove. Whether they would survive up north, she had no idea. But she couldn't bear to leave them behind; she could not bear the thought of them bursting upward, gloriously into blossom, without her, or worse, choked by weeds and devoured by bugs, faltering without her care.

At dawn, she bathed and dressed, twisting her long, dark hair into a loose chignon at the base of her neck. She packed her working clothes, overalls and flannel shirts, a few Sunday dresses, then filled jars and plastic bags with dried tea herbs and two of her favorite porcelain cups. Rose was not a woman overly fond of luxuries, but she knew what she would need for comfort and consolation in a strange place. She also packed her sketch pad, some pens and ink she'd bought in town a few months ago: She had a vague project in mind, a portfolio of botanical sketches, maybe a book. Something to actually do, once she got to Maine.

She locked up her house and climbed into the front seat of her truck, inhaling the greenhouse aroma, mint and hay, the graveyard scent of freshly dug soil. She cast one last glance at her nursery, at the line of lonely greenhouses and plundered yard. She took a deep breath—*Please God, let this be right, the right thing to do*—then turned on the ignition.

How could she even dare to pray? I am the biggest sinner in the world, she thought, giddy with both delight and shame. Falling joyfully toward hell. Choosing eternal death, and yet she felt nothing but heart-pounding girlish anticipation, the sweet, prickly longing of brides and postulants.

At the state line, she was singing softly to herself, but her stomach churned as she approached the tight network of roads surrounding Boston. Once she got past that city, she knew she would not be going back. She imagined the road from Connecticut to Maine as a kind of limbo, a temporary, asphalt connector from one kind of life to another. *It's time*, she told herself, firmly: She was nearly forty, already with strands of gray in the coiled chignon, a web of fine wrinkles at the corners of her eyes. Behind her, to the south, lay her grayish former life—the meandering, so-so business, the early, troubled marriage relieved by five years of calm, chaste widowhood, years filled with gardening and business and church work. And now, an escape to a sort of afterlife. As with death, she had no idea what lay beyond now, what sort of life she would have with Ellis in Maine.

She thought about the phone call that had come only the night before. The summons. So unexpected, a gift, really. She'd never expected to hear from Ellis again. Then suddenly, there was his voice in her ear: a soft tenor, vaguely reedy, formal, tinged with the dropped *R*s and flat *A*s of coastal Maine.

"Where are you?!" she'd demanded. He sounded half a world away, the phone line buzzing with static.

"In Maine." This, in a startled manner, as if it should be perfectly obvious to her.

"What are you *doing* up there?"

"Some reading, some yard work. Walking by the beach, though it's too chilly yet for swimming. I'm thinking of starting a garden."

"*Where?*"

"I have a place here. But I think the soil may be too sandy."

"Ellis, have you . . . Have you gone mad?" It had been a serious inquiry: She really had no idea. He'd answered in an equally serious way: "No, I'm not mad. I'd like to have a garden here. Some landscaping. But I need your help. You're the expert, after all."

"Have you left the priesthood, then?"

"Do you think it's possible to grow anything by the sea? Besides weeds?" His voice had been filled only with deliberately casual curiosity, nothing to indicate any real distress.

"Rose? Are you still there?"

"Yes. I just don't know what to say to you."

"Come up here."

But she did not answer.

"I want you to come. Look at this soil, and tell me if it's worth trying to till."

"Don't they have nurserymen in Maine?"

"I need *you*," he said, softly.

She'd hesitated for only a few seconds. Remembering him in bed, his slender, graceful body, his hands. His fingertips, his tongue, his incredible, intuitive sense of touch.

"I don't know when I can make it," she'd said, hoping her own voice matched his in coolness and deliberation. But at that moment, she had already begun making frenzied plans, wondering which plants she would take with her and which would remain behind.

Now, at the big bridge that spanned the Piscataqua, she almost turned back. She hated driving across bridges, particularly big bridges, bridges over churning water. And what if, she thought, panicking halfway across, Ellis were truly mentally ill? She remembered what life had been like with her husband, ten years of ups and downs, euphoria and blackness, then the awful flood of relief when he committed suicide. Pills and alcohol, not too gruesome. She was almost sick with joy: The freedom she'd felt more than made up for the money the insurance companies denied her. In the rearview mirror, she saw the bridge scooting out behind her. All of a sudden she was in Maine.

She pulled over to consult her map. Once she passed Portland, she would not have far to go. The town of Wainscott Bay appeared at the tip of a small finger curling out into the Atlantic. She bent closer to the map: No, it was actually an island, hugging the mainland tightly, separated from the rest of America by the thinnest thread of blue. Sandy or boggy soil, she found herself thinking. Zone 5 on the frost chart. Her tender Connecticut perennials would perish. She glanced over at them. They were failing fast, wilting, yellowing, drooping—to punish her, she was sure, for the capricious trip, for ripping them from the earth and transporting them to foreign land, where they would only sicken and die. She sighed, pulling back onto the highway, continuing north.

The road to Ellis curved and sloped perilously toward the sea: She never even saw the bridge, but felt the washboard rumble and clacking of the old wood-slat span come right up through her buttocks as the steering wheel vibrated in her hands. She followed a long, flat road through marshes that smelled sweetly of decay, then through a tiny, unremarkable sort of town, punctuated by a white, tall-spired church. Beyond, in the harbor, were spires of a different kind, ships' masts and sailboats. She followed the seaside road to the place Ellis now called home.

She fully expected to find him holed up in some shack-like cottage atop a sand dune. A priest out of a job, certainly out of money. She wouldn't be surprised, and had come armed with her checkbook, a discreet amount of cash. She was completely unprepared for the sight of the huge, rambling Victorian house that stood at the address Ellis had given her. On a hill ending in a cliff, overlooking the sea, it appeared to be a freshly painted soft gray, its fretwork and porch trimmings gleaming white. A boardinghouse for sure, she thought, but then she spied the rural mailbox out front: BARLOWE, it read, in large blocky letters also freshly painted.

Ellis himself sat on the curving, wraparound porch, actually perched on the railing, one long leg drawn up, the other dangling down. He was smoking a cigarette, languidly; his hair, in varying shades of sand, wheat and amber, was blowing about in the brisk wind that came off the bay. She saw his face in profile: pale, fine-boned, the long, patrician nose interrupted by that almost imperceptible bump near the bridge. It was a face that did not readily reveal his true age: She had guessed him to be near her own age, late thirties, but he might be younger or perhaps a bit older. Far from seeming depressed or debilitated—as she had feared and expected—he appeared healthy, well rested, though still on the thin side, clad in a white shirt and fawn-colored trousers. He made no move to greet her, but turned and watched, in a vaguely curious way, as she approached. His coolness unnerved her; she had a wild, sudden urge to turn and flee. Only when she reached the stairs to the porch did he finally jump down off his perch, flicking the cigarette from his fingers. She did not know how to greet him. With a smile, a kiss, an embrace? His eyes met hers briefly: odd, pale eyes, not really blue, but a pearl-gray that often gave his face a lost, empty sort of look. He walked past her and peered into the bed of her truck, silently taking in the rows of potted bushes and plants and flats full of seedlings.

"Ellis?" Her voice was soft, pleading. He turned, abruptly, as if awoken from sleep, and suddenly gave her a sweet, rueful sort of grin. The unexpected smile illuminated his face, which so often was cool, faintly stony in repose. He slid an arm about her shoulders, embracing her now in a warm, but puzzling way: more like the reassuring hug of an older brother or cousin, she thought, than the intense, passionate lover she knew him to be. . . . His chest felt warm, dewy, almost feverish against her cheek and she looked up into his face, astonished at everything she suddenly saw there: a complex mixture of sorrow and confusion, shame and longing, but also a wan sort of joy or pleasure, perhaps relief or gratitude at her presence. His eyes, however, registered only distress—storm-cloud gray, lost, desperate, searching. Nevertheless, he continued to hold her, stroking her arms and back as if comforting, consoling, warming her.

"It's okay, Rose," he whispered. "I'm *fine*."

"*Are* you, Ellis?" she asked, her voice tremulous.

"The plants, the flowers," he went on, haltingly, "I only hope they'll . . . survive, up here. It's so brutal, the wind, the salt, the cold . . ."

She understood. He wasn't ready, yet. To talk.

"This house . . . is it yours?"

"It is now."

"It's your family's house?"

"Yes, but they're gone now, all of them. All dead." He moved away from her and picked up a shovel that had been leaning against the porch. He gave her a worried glance.

"Are you very tired from your trip?"

"Not at all. Just the opposite, in fact."

They went to work right away, working largely in silence: measuring the site, ripping out weeds, digging up the sandy, rocky soil with spades and turning it under. It was no small task; the earth resisted. She watched him, amazed and alarmed by the ceaseless energy and vigor he put into the task of ripping up the sod, displacing shovelfuls of dirt. He labored silently, grimly, hair falling into his face, his mouth a tight, taut line, the back of his shirt spotted with perspiration. He kept his eyes cast down, toward the soil, and for a long time she thought he was deliberately keeping his eyes away from her, avoiding her gaze. Flinching away from her if she happened to brush him or hover too near.

❧

"Rose?"

His voice was low, soft, faintly quizzical. She lay on a chaise on the porch, her eyes closed, utterly exhausted. Too

7

tired to bathe, too weary to even scrape the dirt out from under her fingernails. She was almost asleep, but she sensed him approaching her, warily, catlike. She felt first his breath on her face, then his mouth on hers, his tongue teasing her lower lip. His hands rested on her abdomen, as if waiting for some signal from her to move upward or down; she felt the warmth, the moistness of them through her shirt. She opened her eyes sleepily, helplessly aroused, and met his gaze. The sky above had turned cloudy, threatening, but his eyes, she thought, had deepened in hue to a real blue.

"Help me, Rose," she thought she heard him whisper. "Save me."

And now, in his kisses, the trail of his hands and mouth on her body, she felt, finally, his passion for her, a welcome and almost desperate sort of eagerness that he'd been unable to express earlier in words.

2

Summer, 1995

VISITORS were not rare at Mount Benedetto Abbey, despite its location in remote western Pennsylvania. It was an arduous trip, up through the Allegheny mountain range, along bumpy gravel roads that perilously hugged cliffs and steep hills. It was unusual that a woman would make the journey alone, but not unheard of: A few hardy female souls made the trip each year in search of blessings or comfort, and the monastery had long relaxed the strict rules that once forbade a woman to even cross the abbey's stone threshold.

Still, Lucas, one of the community's younger monks, raced through the corridors to greet the mysterious woman who had turned up in the abbey's visiting parlor. Short, slightly balding, oversize glasses slipping down his nose, Lucas hurried forth, his sandals slapping urgently against the floor tiles. He could not wait to greet this woman, who had asked for, amazingly enough, *Ellis* Barlowe. Not Father Barlowe. Not Father Theophane, the name he'd taken when he'd transferred into their monastic order. But Ellis, his worldly name, the name connected with the life Lucas knew nothing of yet was wildly, desperately curious about. He stopped short of the doorway, poking up his glasses, hoping to get a good look at her first, before he had to break the unhappy news to her.

It was too late: She looked up and spotted him, her face a single plaintive question, a plea. *Where is he?* A woman in late middle age, he guessed, maybe even fifty or sixty. Short, graying brown hair, a no-nonsense style, and a face relatively free of wrinkles and creases, but tanned, freckled. Someone his grandmother might describe as "handsome." A handsome woman in a simple navy linen shift, well wrinkled from what must have been a lengthy drive. Neither slim nor heavy, but there was an odd sensuousness to the curves and fleshiness beneath the dress; her bare arms were muscled and taut, the arms, it seemed, of a much younger woman.

Who was she? A relative? Theo never mentioned any.

"Mrs. Keating?"

She nodded.

"I'm afraid Father can't—"

"Is he ill?" she demanded.

"I don't know how to tell you. Perhaps you should speak to the abbot."

She rose in a shaky way, her face turning pale.

"Dear God," she whispered. "He's not . . . He can't be —*dead*? Is he dead?"

"No!" Lucas shouted in alarm. "Oh, no, no, dear lady. Not at all. I didn't mean to . . . What I'm trying to tell you is, he isn't here."

She frowned. "Where is he, then?" Her voice was now as sharp as a schoolmarm's. Lucas, twisting the fabric of his robes between sweaty hands, said nothing.

"Where'd he go?"

"You should talk to the abbot."

"He's . . . gone? Did he leave the abbey?"

"Honestly, I don't know, ma'am. But he's been gone now for several weeks. We know nothing about it."

She stared at him, incredulous. For a panicky moment, he feared she might actually hit him or lash out in some way. But her face turned reflective and she shook her head slowly.

"Yes," she murmured to herself. "Classic Ellis, running off. Why am I not surprised. But still . . . He seemed so content here, in his letters. He won't reveal much about his inner life, but still, usually there's some clue. But . . . there was nothing. No hints, no darkness, in that last letter. . . ."

Lucas did not respond, thinking it wise not to mention Theo's foul mood in the months before his disappearance. True, Theo was prone to quick anger and taciturn behavior, but his amazing, tireless work in the hospice overrode all that: working through all hours of the night, forsaking sleep and meals, ensuring that his "patients" were comfortable and well tended. Yet in the week before he left, Theo would not go into the hospice wing at all, but stalked about the abbey as if it were a cage, his entire body tight and rigid with some secret, silent anger.

"Are you . . . a friend of Father Theo's?" he ventured. To his surprise, she laughed aloud, a surprisingly bitter laugh.

"A *friend*? Yes, I'm his friend. A friend of *Father*'s." She used the title in an ironic, faintly derisive way; he didn't know what to make of this. "A longtime correspondent. We've been exchanging letters on a regular basis, twice a month, and when he didn't write back, these past two months . . . I knew something was wrong. I just knew it."

"Rose," Lucas whispered. "You're Rose, from Connecticut." He remembered mailing letters for Theo, letters to her. "He said you were a fabulous gardener, and you gave him so much advice, so much help, for his famous herb garden here. He always spoke of you so . . . respectfully." As he said this, he felt a quick stab of envy, remembering the softness that crept into Theo's voice on the odd and infrequent occasions when he mentioned his "friend, the gardener," in Connecticut.

"And yet," Rose murmured, "he did not come to me. If he has indeed run away from being a monk. He did not come to me," she repeated, mournfully, gazing down at the tiled floor. Her eyes suddenly moved back to his face, eyes that were a muted tapestry of gold-green-brown flecks. "Lucas, do you think he's really left, for good?"

"I cannot possibly say." Lucas shrugged, helplessly.

"You're not allowed to?"

"No, it's not that. I simply don't know."

"Was he ill?"

"Not that I knew of. He was amazingly healthy for a man his age."

"Was he unhappy?"

Now Lucas froze. If this Rose was really a close friend of Theo's, hadn't he an obligation to tell her the truth?

"I . . . I'm not sure," he answered, falteringly. Rose smiled in sympathy.

"It's hard to tell, isn't it, with him?"

Lucas smiled back at her, weakly. He was trying to recall the exact words of his last conversation with Theo, the last chance he'd had to talk to Theo before he descended into his dark, angry mood, walling off everyone. He ran it through his mind, searching for clues in Theo's words, gestures, expression. As was usual, Lucas had done most of the talking, and Theo sat listening. He always looked somewhat bored or annoyed, but Lucas had learned this was simply a trick of his face, because suddenly Theo would make some remark that indicated he'd been listening intently all along. Lucas had been complaining about his tasks in the

hospice—he felt sure he was being given the most unpleasant chores, like emptying bedpans and washing the bodies
of the dead, and he was sure he was being punished for
being gay, for making no secret of the fact. And he'd expected Theo to rebuke him for being whiny and complaining, but instead Theo had simply said, calmly, "We'll try to
find more interesting work for you." And he had: he'd put
Lucas to work out in his herb garden, showing him how to
harvest and dry the medicinal plants he used in his teas and
cures. Perhaps Theo knew then he was about to leave; perhaps he was training Lucas to take over his work. Still, he
had the impression that once again Theo had understood
him perfectly, that he had actually read his mind and heart.
Hadn't Theo told him once, gazing right into his eyes, that
he understood perfectly, the torment Lucas was experienc-
ing as a gay man? Lucas had been honest with Theo about
his sexuality, about his urges, but never about his own ram-
pant, fevered attraction to Theo himself. Hadn't he secretly
hoped that by revealing himself so nakedly in conversation
Theo might . . . ? He imagined Theo himself might also be
a lover of men—wishful thinking, perhaps. Theo managed
to be magnificently sympathetic yet properly cool and
chaste at the same time, revealing nothing of his own nature. He had what the older monks called a poker face,
almost classically handsome yet expressionless, eyes like gray
ice, and yet Lucas always imagined some cauldron bubbling
away inside him, a secret, anguished, passionate man hidden
beneath the iceberg facade. A secret, tortured early life that
had infused wisdom and perspective into his calm, later
years as a monk.

But now, he was gone! Where? Lucas thought, his own
anguish almost unbearable. Why? He gazed at the sad, but
seemingly resigned, motherly woman before him, and his
hand suddenly darted out to take hers. Not necessarily in
sympathy for her, but for his own desperate comfort.

3

"**A**ND here is sage. For sore throats and colds." Rose plucked one of the spear-shaped leaves and handed it to him. Ellis sniffed at it and gave her an amused, skeptical grin, as if she were telling him fairy tales, charming but not really true.

"And rosemary—"

"For remembrance," he added, remembering his Shakespeare.

"Here's chamomile. For your headache tea."

"What's this, this little blue plant you have back here?"

"Rue," she replied, remembering too late its religious significance, the herb of grace, of sinners and repentance. She went to snatch it, to rip it from the soil, but he caught her hand. "Don't," he murmured. "We may need it for something."

She blinked, astounded by this unexpected tenderness when she might have expected irritation or annoyance from him. She had still not quite adjusted to being with him.

She was still struggling with the silences, the long periods when he would not speak, or left her to go walking on the beach alone. At first the silences felt hurtful to her, cold, exclusionary, but she was beginning to understand they had nothing to do with her. When they worked together in the garden without speaking, she would sometimes catch him gazing at her, regarding her with a sort of quiet amazement. And, she thought, gratitude.

After gardening, he begged her not to wash up so quickly, drawing her to bed before she could escape to the bath. He liked her flushed and dusty and gamy with sweat, arms streaked with clay and humus; he took a peculiar erotic pleasure in it. She couldn't quite understand it, having somehow imagined him to be a fastidious sort of man. Perhaps, she thought, that was a trick of her brain: In her mind's eye, she still saw him in his black suit and pristine white collar, hands stuck sulkily in the pockets of his coat.

This was her very first image of him, the morning they first met, in October, a year and a half before: she on her knees in front of the church, with Sissie Neel, planting tulip bulbs with hands full of bonemeal. The monsignor brought him by. "Look, here's the new priest." She was struck immediately by the washed-out color of his eyes that made him seem to be one of those vacant, lackluster priests unable to move beyond a certain point in their career. But then she saw the intelligent, sardonic slant of his mouth, and this troubled her: that, and the faint, almost foreign, thrill of physical attraction. He said nothing, but offered his hand. She looked down at her own, grimy and caked with dirt, then curled it into a tight ball.

"Ooooh," Sissie winced, when he was out of sight. "He's going to be a cold fish, I can tell. Did you see those *eyes*?"

He was, thought Rose, and sometimes he wasn't. Rose had had little experience with men: only her husband of ten years and a brief, unhappy relationship before him. From these two men, she learned that sex was a brutal thing to be avoided or endured, and any pleasure she felt was a freakish accident. With Ellis she understood, finally, what it was all about between men and women.

All the magic, she thought, lay in his touch: slow, deliberate, teasing. His mouth and tongue, the pads of his fingers, seemed possessed of an unerring intuition, knowing the precise amount of pressure or friction to apply to the tips of her breasts. When he kissed her, in his long, slow, deliberate way, she imagined him trying to memorize with his own mouth the shape and texture of hers; he then shocked her by sliding his lips down her body, burrowing between her legs, committing to memory the delicate, secret shape of her sex. When they made love, those first few weeks, he always withdrew from her with a small, anguished cry, spilling his milky seed onto her abdomen. Then, to her utter astonishment, he would lick her clean, like a sly cat lapping spilt cream off the floor. He'd laugh and kiss her on the mouth, so she tasted the bitter, salty taste of him, on his lips. It struck her as perverse, yet unbearably arousing; and so she waited nearly two weeks before telling him his withdrawal was completely unnecessary, because the doctors had told her she was sterile, incapable of conceiving a child.

She loved his body, loved the almost delicate slenderness of it; she loved feeling his ribs, his bones beneath the pale, smooth flesh, the hairless chest, pale pink nipples that hardened into pebbles when she grazed them and then, in its nest of wiry gold hair, his smooth circumcised member, not freakishly long, but thick, with a defiant leftward tilt when erect. They made love every night during those first few weeks of late spring and early summer, sometimes twice, and again in the morning; and even then she often awoke, the bedsprings gently shaking beneath them, to find him vigorously pleasuring himself. This worried her faintly, this insatiable streak, this explosion of libido. Perhaps it was understandable, she thought, after so many years of celibacy. But how could a supposedly celibate man make love so skillfully, so expertly? She didn't dare ask him yet. There was so much about him she did not know.

The early weeks of their relationship passed, a blur of gardening and feverish sex. They did not talk much, those first weeks: She held her tongue, desperately curious but waiting for some cue from him to probe deeper, while he made it clear—by turning away or changing the subject—that certain topics were off-limits, not yet open to discussion: his past, his career in the Church, his spiritual status, his future, his own family. When Rose asked him, as carefully as she could manage, about his father and mother, she was astonished to see him actually wince, his eyes darting away from her. But he'd remained silent and said nothing about them.

The garden was their sanctuary, safe ground; here they could talk easily and innocuously about the soil, about weather and the threat of Japanese beetles. They continued to toil, ripping up the estate's thin sod for various plots: showy perennials out front, the herb garden, or "pharmacy," as Ellis referred to it, by the side, under the porch. Out back, overlooking the sea, a small four-by-eight bed for vegetables filled with purchased soil from the mainland, but supplemented with chopped algae and sea plants they collected from the water's edge.

When one of his headaches came on, as they did with startling regularity—once a week, often twice—Rose brewed his healing tea. It was a poignant ritual for her. Sifting in the dried chamomile blossoms, the ground-up willow and other bits of greenery, twigs and roots, she sighed, inhaling the tangible, sweetly scented reminders of the forest and garden she'd left behind. She brought the steaming brew to Ellis, who would be stretched, motionless, on the sofa or the chaise lounge on the porch, pale as death, a cool washcloth across his eyes. At her approach, the creak of her footsteps, he would hold his hands out, helplessly, for her. She fed him the tea as she might feed a sick child, nestled against him, helping him sit up, carefully tilting the porcelain cup against his lips, distressed, as always, at how the pain transformed, contorted his face. Yet he never spoke of it or described it to her, nor complained or moaned, though a bad attack could last the better part of a day, and sometimes into the next. She knew, even when he was asleep, when it was over: Suddenly his face was relaxed again, with some color, his breathing normal.

They filled their days in the garden. If it rained, she took out her sketch pad and worked on her plant drawings. Sometimes Ellis sat and silently watched her draw, or he went off to read. He was making his way through Will and Ariel Durant's Story of Civilization series. He'd gone and bought all the volumes at once and kept them in a big stack beside his wicker chair on the porch. He seemed absorbed, even comforted, by this vast overview of human history, but always seemed faintly dazed, disoriented, after a long stretch of reading, blinking as if startled to find himself back on the coast of Maine in the twentieth century. They might well be in another century, some distant alien land, she thought, so remote and cut off were they from the rest of the world, from modern life. They did not even have a radio, let alone a TV.

She was stunned when she heard the telephone ring for the very first time. She hadn't even realized Ellis had a phone, and it took her some time to locate it. As it happened, he was out, taking a walk along the beach as he did every evening: one of those hurried, agitated strolls he took along the edge of the surf, barefoot, as if he had a specific and urgent destination in mind, though Rose could not imagine what.

She picked up the phone, immensely curious about who might be on the other end. Wrong number, maybe.

"Is Father Barlowe there?" a male voice barked tersely. She instantly recognized the voice of her old pastor from St. Cyril's parish.

"No," she murmured in a low voice, terrified he would recognize her voice. How many committees had she served on, how many church suppers had she prepared? She wasn't one of those parishioners a pastor saw only once a year.

"Will he be in soon?"

"I don't know."

"It's urgent that I speak with him. Is this a relation of his?" Before she could answer, he continued. "Tell him we're very worried about him. Tell him to call us, we can talk about it. This was so unexpected, this . . . this abrupt departure of his. Father Ellis hides a lot from us, but he never let on he was unhappy or troubled. And he was doing such a superb job here. Talk in the diocese was that he was about to be given a parish of his own, elevated to monsignor. Seventeen years a priest: How can he give it up so easily?"

She was stunned to hear all this, but said nothing.

"All the best ones, leaving now. These new changes in the Church. It's too much, too sudden."

She set the receiver down, quickly.

Ellis arrived home some time later, amid darkening skies and a fierce wind that clattered the screened porch door: He threw an anxious glance back at the storm that had chased him home. She approached him, warily.

"You had a phone call earlier this evening. When you were out taking your walk."

He raised his eyebrows, but said nothing.

"It was the monsignor from St. Cyril's."

"What did he want?" he asked in an amazingly casual

way, as if he'd just returned from a hospital call or the Rosary Society's social. She stared at him in confusion.

"Ellis, I had no idea you'd been a priest for so long. Seventeen years? You're older than I thought you were."

"What did he *want*, Rose?" There was an edge in his voice now.

"I really don't know anything about you. When you come right down to it, I'm living with a complete stranger —Ellis, don't—"

He walked away from her, as if insulted. She hurried after him, the porch door rattling away, a stacatto of rain hitting the windows. "We should really talk about this, Ellis. We need to *talk*—"

He turned to her, and she saw, in his forehead, a tight crease between his eyes, a hint of the crippling migraine about to descend. "What did he say? Just tell me his exact words."

"What do you think he said? He wants you back, he wants to know why you left. Didn't you give him any clue, leave a note? Did you think someone from the Church wouldn't make an attempt to find you, to talk to you?"

"Was he angry?"

"No, I think he's worried. You upset him terribly. I think you must talk to him, Ellis. Clear the air."

He turned his attention back to the dark storm; sheets of rain were now streaking down the glass. "I can't. I don't have an explanation for him yet."

"But he'll call back. Someone will call back—"

To her astonishment, he stalked over to the telephone and swiftly disconnected it from the wall.

"Ellis!" she cried, feeling a spurt of anger and dismay. "You're acting like a coward. Why can't you face up to this like a man?"

He paled, as if she'd struck him across the face.

"Is that how you think of me?"

"I don't know what to think of you. But I can't go on here with you, being silent, not questioning, not talking—"

"I *can't* talk about it!" he shouted. "If I *could* talk about it, I wouldn't have done it. I wouldn't have left! I wouldn't have abandoned my parish, the only real kind of life I've ever known, my family—"

She stared at him. "What family?"

"I don't mean relations. I meant the Church . . . was my family." His face contorted in true misery now.

"My God," she murmured. "What did your family . . . your *real* family . . . *do* to you?"

His hands went to his temples, rubbing them, massaging them. He seemed to be trying to calm himself, to compose himself.

"Rose, none of this . . . has anything to do with you. I don't want you to be involved in it, it's something I have to deal with on my own. If you want to stay on with me, fine, but I must have *peace*. I can't have this poking and probing. I won't have it. It has nothing at all to do with you."

The words hit her with the intensity of the outdoor storm: She felt almost physical pain on hearing them. It had nothing to do with her. He had not left the priesthood out of any passion or longing for her. *It had nothing to do with her.* She was only a bystander, a quick hostage he'd manage to grab along the way. She turned and walked into the bedroom they shared together and threw her suitcase onto the bed. She felt tears coming, and she began to pack, rushing to pack faster, before her eyes spilled over and she wouldn't be able to stop crying. I can't stay, she thought: How can I stay under such conditions? She was struggling, simultaneously, to close her suitcase and pull it off the bed, when suddenly it was whisked out of her hands. Ellis then crouched down, peering up into her face with the incredulous hurt of a small boy.

"You're not leaving? Not this minute?"

"You told me to."

"I did not. I only said—"

"I know what you said. And I can't stop asking questions. I need to know about you, Ellis, all about you, if I'm to stay with you. I don't want to hurt you, I only want to understand."

"So do I," he whispered.

"Then talk to me."

He shook his head. "I'm sorry, Rose. I'm so sorry to involve you in all this. I had no right to ask you to give up everything, to come here to me—"

"Do you want me to stay?"

He bowed his head, shielding his face completely from her. The thunder outside was now rumbling away, the rain still a muted roar, enveloping the house. She saw his fingers dig into his face and heard a soblike intake of breath, as the muscles of his neck tightened, constricted. "Ellis—?" She pulled his hand away from his face, and he lifted his gray-iceberg eyes to her, now wet, overflowing with tears.

"I don't know if I can do it, Rose," he whispered.

"What? Do what?" Her own hands instinctively went to stroke his face, his hair; she moved closer to comfort him in a more substantial way, holding him tightly. He leaned into her, burrowing his face into her neck, her shoulder; she felt his tears seeping through the fabric of her shirt.

"Be . . . normal. An ordinary sort of . . . man." He wiped his eyes. "I don't know if there's any kind of life for me here. Or anywhere."

She hugged him more tightly, feeling deeply moved and heartsick, all at once. "Do you *want* me to stay, Ellis?"

He nodded against her shoulder.

"I need to hear it," she whispered. "Tell me."

"Please," he whispered into her shoulder, "I need you. Don't leave me now."

4

"I WISH you'd spoken to me before talking with Brother Lucas." The abbot addressed her politely, even pleasantly, but Rose heard a paternal sort of reprimand behind his words, which made her bristle. A rosy, roly-poly sort of man, he reminded her of the chubby ceramic monks one often saw for sale at flea markets and junk shops. She wondered how Ellis got along with him. "Father Barlowe has not abandoned us, nor has he disappeared under mysterious circumstances. In fact, I know *exactly* where he is."

But you're not going to tell me, thought Rose. Nevertheless, she sat before the abbot in an attentive, ladylike way, her hands folded, waiting for him to continue.

"He checks in with us on a regular basis. We do not, as a rule, allow vacations or sabbaticals, and of course, a priest can never take a sabbatical from his vows. But when Theo asked me for this little bit of time away as a special favor, I felt I couldn't refuse him. He is a pillar of our community, an immensely valuable man here. I didn't approve of the idea, but I decided to let him go, in the hope he would return spiritually and emotionally stronger. He has a difficult job, caring for the terminally ill. Those with cancer and failing hearts, and now AIDS patients who've begun filtering in." He paused. "I don't know what we'd do without him."

Rose saw, out of the corner of her eye, a flash of gray by the door, the hem of a robe, a sandaled foot, then a glimpse of a worried, anxious face: Lucas, the little monk she'd spoken to just moments before. What a strange boy, she thought. He reminded her a little, physically, of her youngest son, Tommy, who was mentally retarded but a wizard with the till, short and slight but happy to dig splendid trenches and holes for arborvitae. Both monk and son had rounded faces, with the same sort of sweet, poignantly baffled expression, as if life were some impenetrable, tragic puzzle they could never hope to figure out.

"To protect Theo's privacy, I did not discuss the matter with the other monks. In any case, he will be back soon enough and can explain his absence to them if he wishes. And I don't want the others to be requesting vacations now, either."

"When do you expect him back?"

Now the abbot hesitated. "Soon," he said, his round face uncertain. Rose leaned forward.

"Look, I know where he is. Just confirm it for me."

The abbot blinked, perhaps in surprise or indignation. "He requested a small stipend and the use of a car. That's all I can tell you. I am sorry you missed him, Mrs. Keating." He stood up, and she understood she was being dismissed. "But we can tell him you were here. Perhaps you'd like to leave a note."

"No, no," she said, pleasantly. "I expect I might encounter him eventually on my travels. And I'll tell him you sent your regards." She departed swiftly, grabbing a startled Lucas's arm on the way out.

"Before I leave, can you show me his garden? I've heard all about it in his letters, and I've imagined it so many times. Can I see it? Would it be allowed?"

Lucas led her outside to a small plot, which sat nestled in the L formed by a stark, modern addition conjoined to the traditional stone abbey. He gazed up at the sterile, white boxlike addition. "That's the new infirmary-hospice wing. They had to expand when men started coming to us from the outside. We don't turn anyone away. Father Theo built it. I mean, he came up with the financing, somehow."

"I did wonder," Rose said slowly, "what he did with all his money." She squinted at the building. "God, it's ugly."

"It's a haven," Lucas murmured. "A place of peace for men who have lost hope." But his voice lacked enthusiasm, as if he were reciting from memory.

"He wasn't just treating people with herbs, was he? This wasn't one of those New Age quackery joints—"

"No, no. Theo had enormous faith in modern medicine. The herbs are just for easing symptoms. In fact, Theo said they really had more of a psychological effect than a true medicinal one. He was really a *brilliant* man," Lucas gushed, then suddenly blushed. "But I guess you know that."

Rose didn't answer. She was studying the garden. She sighed, distressed.

"Brick paths in the shape of a cross. Such a cliché. I wouldn't expect Ellis to be overly concerned with design. But still, I thought it would be . . . I don't know, larger, more magnificent somehow. The way he described it! It's a mess, really, it needs a sound weeding, and how can you tell where anything is?"

"Theo knew where everything was."

"I hope so." Suddenly, she laughed in delight. "Look

here, at this bush. Agnus-castus. This is from my nursery! Oh, it's doing magnificently here, better than it would ever do in Connecticut." She turned to Lucas. "Ellis really wanted it. It's a very traditional monastic herb. He said that ancient monks would slip it into their breeches to preserve their chastity."

Lucas blushed again. She wondered if she'd embarrassed him.

"Do you really know where he is?" he asked, shyly.

"I'm not sure," Rose answered softly, ruefully. "I let the abbot think that I did, but truthfully, I'm not altogether sure. I'm really hurt that he didn't come to Connecticut to see me"—the truth was, she was devastated, having believed for years and years that Ellis would indeed leave the monastery and come back to her—"but . . . there is another place he could be. His home."

"He's from Maine or New Hampshire, isn't he? I could tell by the slight accent he has. Do you think that's where he went?"

Rose sighed. "He'd have no reason to. He has no family there, nothing left there, except . . . memories. But not good ones, I'm afraid." For a long moment, she stared up at the stone facade of the monastery, wishing she could see what had held Ellis there for so many years, for decades—and what had driven him out. For she was not at all reassured by the abbot's smooth words. She was certain that Ellis had left Mount Benedetto for good.

She turned to Lucas and took his hand. "Thank you. . . . You've been very kind, very patient with a crazy old lady."

"Not at all," Lucas stammered. "I . . . I'm happy to have met you. Someone from Theo's . . . past." The desperate look in his eyes told Rose that he yearned to know more, but dared not ask. "If you walk around this building, you'll end up back in the parking lot." And abruptly, he picked up his robes and hurried off, like a scared gray rabbit.

She lingered for a moment in Ellis's garden and shut her eyes, inhaling the vaguely minty aroma of herbs wafting in the wind. *Where are you?* she asked silently. *And what is this need I have to see you again, after so many years?* She shook her head: It was absurd, completely irrational, this flare-up of longing and yearning for him. Completely irrational at her age, but then her connection to him had never been rational or even sane. Her love for him had been something wild and unearthly, and even thirty years with another man, filled with children and farming and business, had been unable to extinguish it entirely, fed as it was—feebly—by the chaste, careful correspondence she and Ellis had maintained over the years. She pulled from her purse her last letter from him, written here, perhaps in this very spot. In it he complained about his rosemary and his thyme growing out of bounds, and that his hyssop seemed to have lost its effectiveness. But how grateful he was for the agnus-castus and all the other rare herbs she had provided for him—*You shall know that you have had a hand in helping the poor, ill men here, in giving life to these humble plants and sharing them with me.* It amused her that Ellis wrote in such a formal, stilted, even pretentious manner so unlike his speech. His speech, which she could barely remember now. She could not quite remember what his voice sounded like, only bits of the soft, coastal-Maine drawl. Would she even recognize him if she saw him again?

Two months ago, the letters had stopped. That last connection with him had been snipped, severed. It was something serious: She knew it. And she sensed that somewhere, wherever he was, he needed her.

She walked resolutely back to the parking lot through the grass along the perimeter of the monastery, her heels sinking into the earth. She was thinking of more basic matters now. How long would it take her to drive to Maine? Should she stop at home, in Connecticut, first? Check on

Mandy and Tommy and the grandkids, make sure the nursery hadn't collapsed?

But as she began to open the door of her old pickup truck, she was startled by a garbled sort of shout. She looked and saw, to her astonishment, the monk Lucas—out of his robes and wearing jeans and an oversize brown sweater—running toward her.

"Rose," he gasped. "Take me. Take me with you!"

"I can't!" she cried. "Lucas, I couldn't possibly—"

"Please. I can't stay here without him. Let me come, help you look."

"I don't need any help," she said firmly, but he jumped into the cab of her truck and planted himself stubbornly in the front seat.

"Get *out*! I don't need to deal with this right now, young man."

"Please, Rose. *Please*." He clasped his hands together in a prayerful way. "At least just take me away from here. I can't be here any longer."

She stared at him: Even with the thinning hair and glasses, the face pinched with desperation, he was an appealing, attractive sort of boy, she thought. But what in the world would she do with him? She sighed.

"All right. Buckle that seat belt."

He struggled to comply, eagerly, awkwardly, and ultimately unsuccessfully: She watched him for a while, awash with pity and dismay, then finally leaned over and strapped him in soundly.

 **5**

B Y the middle of June, the seedlings and perennials and herbs Rose had brought from Connecticut had been firmly planted in the sandy Maine soil of the Barlowe estate. Those that survived the journey quivered bravely in the breezes off the sea. As she expected, many perished, but she was heartened, overjoyed to see her foxglove buds swelling, the stalks pushing upward; the thyme burst into tiny lavender flowers and the Greek oregano sprawled comfortably along the rounded, ocean-smoothed stones Ellis brought up from the edge of the surf to frame the herb garden. She made her first real foray off the property, to a nursery-farm called Keating's, where she bought some cheerful marigolds, geraniums and zinnias to add color to their still-bare plots.

Ellis decided he could not have enough privacy. Muttering darkly about "summer people" coming, he erected, with his own hands, a wooden fence along the southern border of his property, then disguised it with a mixed planting of yew, hemlock and arborvitae. Rose ordered the shrubs from Keating's, wondering where the money for this extravagant planting was coming from. But somehow Ellis always managed to have money without ever taking anything from her.

She assisted Ellis as he dug great holes for the shrubs and refilled them partially with peat moss and other organic material.

"I suppose you expect to be here for a long time," she remarked, but he seemed not to hear her. He was in his solemn but vigorous work mode, shirtless, grimly sweating as he eased unwieldy evergreens into the holes he'd dug. He'd grown tan and muscled in his weeks here, his hair even fairer, more and more wonderfully attractive to her. When he paused for a brief break, she pointed at the line of windows on the second floor of his house.

"What's upstairs in your mansion? Are there more bedrooms?"

He did not even look. "It's closed off. There was a problem with bats and rodents coming down. It was easier just to seal it off."

"You could fix it up. You could build a staircase to that little balcony there—"

"No," he murmured, looking down into the soil.

"You could rent the upstairs—"

"I don't need to," he snapped. He wiped his face with a towel. "I don't want anyone else here."

He seemed cross with her now, but she knew it wouldn't last. A few more hours of work would turn him oddly amorous again. She plunged her own arms deep into the dirt and composted manure, knowing that it would only add to her allure for him later on.

In bed, he was in a sweeter mood. His passion for her spent, and pleasantly exhausted from his day of work, he lay with his arms loosely wrapped about her, gazing up at the window above the bed they shared.

"No shadows on the moon tonight," he murmured.

"What was that?"

"Ever read Dante?" he asked her.

Rose, whose formal education ended with her graduation from high school, simply shrugged.

"In *The Divine Comedy*, Dante asks Beatrice, his guide through the afterlife, about the shadows on the face of the moon." The teacher in him seemed to emerge in a pleasant, glowing way, his graceful hands caressing an imaginary orb. "The first circle of heaven, a place reserved for religious unable to keep their vows. You're not much of a romantic, are you? So practical, but surely that must appeal to your Irish, old-maid sensibilities." He was mocking her, but in a curiously sweet way. She could actually hear the affection in his voice. He had not, as she feared, grown tired of her in these past few weeks, but had begun to address her with increasing warmth.

"My God," she murmured, with a chuckle. "You know absolutely nothing about me."

"I don't," he said, in a melancholy way. "We really are strangers to each other, aren't we?"

"We are," she whispered, drawing closer to him.

"Are you a romantic, after all?"

"I'm neither Irish, nor an old maid. Connolly was my husband's name." It gave her a peculiar thrill to say this; it felt like a boast. *There was someone, before you.*

He nodded. "So you were married. I should have realized, considering your skill and ease in the bedroom."

"My parents were born in the Soviet Union."

"Oh, stop it," he laughed, in delight. "Don't tell me crazy stories. Are you a spy?"

"They were Jews. Ukrainian Jews."

"And that's where you got your classic Celtic features? Those eyes, those freckles, that marvelous auburn hair with the glint of fire in it?"

"Well, don't believe me, then."

"How did you end up a Catholic—widow? Divorcée? On a Connecticut farm?"

"I don't know how they got to the United States. Or how they ended up in Hartford—that's where I was born. The nuns in the orphanage where I grew up told me they were from Odessa. And that I had a Jewish last name."

"You didn't know them at all."

"No, no. I don't know what happened to my father. My mother was apparently in the final stages of cancer when she left me with the nuns. I do think about her from time to time, alone in a strange land, dying an excruciating death and with such a young child . . . I was only two, a toddler, when she died. From then on, I had only the nuns."

"Oh, Rose," he murmured into her shoulder. She felt slightly mortified by the odd, sudden spurt of sympathy.

"Don't feel sorry for me. I didn't have a bad childhood. It was hard, and lonely at times, but good preparation . . . excellent preparation for life. I never had any illusions about myself and my future. I just learned to work hard and not want anything too badly."

"What was your husband like?" He seemed genuinely curious.

"He was a farmer. He had a big farm in Wisterville. I went out with a busload of other girls to work in his fields. He took a fancy to me. I don't know why."

"But you didn't love him."

"He was a good man," she replied, stiffly. "It was a fine marriage." She was lying now, deceiving him, but she couldn't bear to share the truth with him yet, fearing it would demean her in his eyes. Surely he'd think the fault of the bad marriage, her husband's madness, was hers. She knew it wasn't so, but she also knew people always suspected and blamed the wife.

"Yet, no children," he murmured.

"I told you, I can't have them."

"Did you want them?"

She considered this. Once the doctor's verdict came in, she had simply accepted it and had not allowed herself to yearn or pine for what was impossible, off-limits to her. But she did feel, every so often, an unmistakable surge of envy, or loss, whenever she spotted a young mother pushing a carriage, or a crowd of eager children tumbling out of a school bus.

"Well, of course," she murmured. "What kind of woman doesn't want children?"

"Some women are better off without them." He sounded melancholy. She looked into his face.

"Was that some reference to your own mother?"

"Are you a psychoanalyst now?"

"You never talk about—"

"Come here." He slid his hand between her thighs, sliding his fingers into her, working them in the way that made her breath catch in her throat, making her forget her questions.

But afterward he still seemed restless.

"I'm going out. For a walk."

"What? At this hour?" She sat up in alarm. He gently pushed her back down onto the bed. "Go to sleep, Rose. Please, don't worry. I'll be back soon."

When he was gone, she left the bed, slid into her robe and crept out into the hallway. Silently, stealthily, she climbed the stairs, clutching a flashlight. Sure enough, the door at the top of the stairs was locked tight, nailed firmly shut. She knelt down on the landing and peered through a small gap between door and floor: She tried to squeeze the circle of light in through the slit of dark, but could make out little but the edge of an old Oriental carpet runner. Whatever secrets the upstairs floor held about Ellis were safe behind the nailed door, safe in the dark.

6

SPEEDING toward Harrisburg, Pennsylvania, Rose cast a nervous glance at her passenger, the runaway monk, who'd said virtually nothing since they'd left Mount Benedetto together. True, she'd been annoyed with him—still upset, worried sick over Ellis—and had gruffly rebuffed his initial feeble attempts to converse with her, but she felt herself beginning to soften after a couple of hours on the road. She even felt some curiosity about him. She wondered about his relationship to Ellis: Friend? Student? Or merely an admirer?

"This is the longest trip I've ever made," she murmured. "Who'd have thought Pennsylvania was so large?"

"How long will it take us to get to Maine?" Lucas asked, almost eagerly, as if sensing her warming mood.

"Oh, I can't drive to Maine from here. I have to go home to Connecticut first. I have to check on the business and family and all. I shouldn't have made this crazy trip. I really don't have the time for it. It's not like I'm some lonely old crone with nothing else to do, you know."

"I'm from Connecticut, too," he ventured. She glanced at him.

"Whereabouts?"

"Near Greenwich."

Well-to-do, she thought. "Will you be contacting your folks, then?"

"I . . . I don't know if I can. I guess the abbot will probably call them and . . . my father will be . . . Oh, I'm not sure I can go back there."

"You should probably at least call. Especially since they'll be near. I know I always want to know what my children are up to, no matter what."

"My dad predicted I would drop out of the monastery. It's like I followed his orders. He'll be furious that I left, though. He always said I could never stick to anything. And he'll be embarrassed now, when he plays golf with his friend the bishop, who always asks about me."

"An important man, your father?"

"He's a lawyer, he handles a lot of work for the diocese. He ran for office a few years back. For the House of Representatives, but he lost in the primary. My older brothers are lawyers, too, and what he wanted for me was to become a priest. Every fine Irish-Catholic family in New England has to have one, you know." Suddenly, he laughed, a delighted, sly-child's giggle. "Boy, was he ticked off when I went into the monastery! I went into the religious life, but it wasn't *his* kind of religious life. It was like a sort of victory for me. But that's not the reason I went in," he added, quickly.

"Why did you?" Rose asked, in a casual way.

"Because I thought I had the vocation for it. The call."

"But you don't?"

"I don't know. You'd think after ten years I'd be certain of it, but I seem to grow less certain each day. I was so young when I went in, only eighteen. . . . How could I have known then what I would want for the rest of my life?" He let a few dark miles pass. "How many children do you have, Rose?"

"Three. All late-in-life babies, but all grown now. Mandy, my oldest—she's home with me again, things didn't work out with her live-in boyfriend. Henry—Hank—my middle boy, is married, has a farm of his own, but still helps me with the business. He has two gorgeous little girls, with Grandpa's red hair. Spoiled somewhat, but that's the mother's doing. And Tommy, my baby. He's retarded, but you'd never know it. He's the hardest worker I ever had. Still, I worry about him, worry about how he'll do after I'm gone."

"Gone? You mean, gone to Maine, to find Theo?"

"I meant, when I'm dead." She chuckled, grimly.

"You're not dying, are you, Rose?" Lucas asked, with some concern.

"Not that I know of. Oh, I've had my problems over the years. Sicknesses and operations and now I have to watch my blood pressure, the doctor says. Have to keep my weight down. Nothing really serious, yet. But when you get up into my age, there isn't a whole lot of sand left in the hourglass. It's only a matter of time before something comes along. It makes you think about the passage of time, how swiftly it all goes by. . . ."

"When did your husband pass away?"

"He didn't. Did I say he did?"

"No, no, I'm sorry, but I somehow thought—"

"It's all right. I know what you meant. You'd expect a good husband to accompany his wife on such an arduous journey. But my husband's not in any kind of shape to travel. He had a massive stroke about two years ago. He

37

just never really recovered. We have him at home now, but he's bedridden, he really isn't . . . He's really not *living* at all, if you know what I mean."

"I am so sorry, Rose."

"Well, that's life." She drove a bit farther. "I hope you don't think I'm callous or uncaring. The truth is, I've already mourned for Burt, and I've accepted the end of him. I never thought it would take so long. But it's true, it takes some people years to die. I guess we're all dying, when you think about it; we're all heading in that same direction anyway."

"What a cheerful thought," Lucas murmured. Rose laughed again.

"A long drive in the dark will do that to you. Makes you feel morose and sorry for yourself." She paused. "I have to admit, it's good having a companion for going back. Otherwise I'd be driving myself crazy, thinking about Ellis."

"I could drive for a while."

"*Can* you?"

"I think I remember how. It's probably been about ten years or so . . ."

"Never mind. I think we should probably stop for the night. Find a motel . . . I guess I could spring for two rooms."

"You needn't worry about me, Rose. I wouldn't bother you in any way," said Lucas in a formal, serious manner that almost made her laugh again. She glanced over at him.

"Forgive me for being blunt, but you're *gay*, aren't you?"

He looked startled and hurt. "Is it so obvious?"

"No, not really. Well, yes, in a way. I can't explain it. I got this sense . . . about the way you spoke of Theo—I mean Ellis—just made me think—"

"Let me drive, Rose. I can do it, I know I can." She eased the truck onto the shoulder of the highway, and they switched sides. He seemed surprisingly at ease behind the wheel, pulling expertly back out into traffic.

"Theo was my mentor, my teacher," he explained, clutching the steering wheel tightly. "And yes, I admired him enormously and came to love him . . . but it's not what you think, we weren't . . . I wasn't . . . It was chaste, *purely* platonic. Anyway, Theo was only barely aware of my existence. There were others at the monastery who were his favorites."

"His favorites? Watch that truck on your side there."

"I see it. Not other monks, but his patients. Maybe it was my imagination, but I always felt Theo cared more for his patients than anyone else. It was like you had to be dying to earn his respect and admiration."

"That's an odd comment," said Rose. "And it doesn't sound like the Theo I know. Oh, drat! Now you have me calling him that!"

"That's his name, Rose. Theophane. 'Lover of God.' "

"I have a feeling he's reverted back to Ellis."

"Were *you* in love with him?" Lucas asked suddenly, as if emboldened by his new status as a pickup truck driver. For a long time she didn't answer.

"Yes," she answered, carefully. "I suppose I can confess to that."

"Ah, but you were married to someone else," Lucas murmured, clearly captured by the tragedy of it all.

"It was complicated, let's leave it at that."

"Were you . . ." He broke off, unable to ask the question. *Were you lovers?* He wasn't sure he wanted to hear the answer, wasn't sure he wanted to be forced to revise his image of Theo from chaste homosexual to sinning heterosexual. To his enormous relief, Rose broke in with a benign comment:

"Ellis and my husband are related. They are cousins."

"Oh, oh, I get it."

"No, I don't think you do." She chuckled, ruefully.

"You met Theo after you married your husband?"

"Actually, it was the other way around. I'd known Ellis for a while before I met Burt. My, you're curious. I'm going to start asking *you* a lot of questions."

"I just need to know, how did you first meet Theo? How did you come to know him? What was his life like . . . *before*. Before us, before Benedetto?"

"Look, there's a Dunkin' Donuts at this next exit. If we're going to drive all night, we may as well fortify ourselves with that wonderful coffee of theirs."

"Okay." Lucas drove a little faster, fueled by curiosity and longing, hoping the answers to some of his questions would come in the donut shop by the edge of the interstate.

7

"WE'RE going sailing," Ellis announced to her one day, showing up at breakfast dressed entirely in white. She stared at him, dumbfounded. "Come on." He laughed, pulling her out of her chair. "No work today. Go put on a bathing suit, some shorts."

"You don't have a boat, do you?"

"No," he replied, with a sly smile. "I'm going to borrow one."

They traveled down to the town marina. Rose, having neither a bathing suit nor shorts, was forced to cut off the legs of her dingiest jeans and tie the tails of a sleeveless blouse under her bosom; she felt like a poor hillbilly relation of Ellis's. He seemed cool, sleek, unruffled in his white garb, his fair hair blowing in the breeze. He walked up and down the dock, studying the various sailing vessels before seeming to decide on one in particular. He leapt onto it and signaled for Rose to join him.

"Ellis—" she murmured, in a warning way. "Whose boat is that?"

"Don't worry, it belongs to a friend."

"A friend?" Since when, she thought, does he have a friend in this town? He hadn't mentioned any.

"Oh, come on, Rose!" He seemed amused by her reluctance.

"Ellis, I've never been on a boat before."

He held his hand out for hers and pulled; she landed against him with a great thud that sent the entire vessel aquiver. He laughed in a delighted, cheery way, a new sound to her ears. "Just sit," he told her. "I'll do all the work." She watched him fiddle with ropes and sails; she had no idea what he was doing. Sailing was as mysterious to her as religion. Yet the boat was moving, skimming along the water as, she supposed, it should. Still, she cowered down, clinging tightly to the side, shuddering with each unexpected lurch and sway. She glanced up at her lover, who seemed transformed. There was something childlike in his happiness, his clear delight in maneuvering the boat and being on the sea. Gone was the tightness, the grimness that accompanied his gardening chores: If that work was his penance, then this work—the task of keeping the boat afloat, moving it from one spot to another—was an indulgence, a reward. He was actually humming.

"It's been a while. Haven't lost my skills yet." He seemed quite pleased with himself.

"Whose boat is this, Ellis?" she asked, in a voice faintly dark with suspicion. He heard it and laughed.

"It belongs to a woman I know. Edna."

She felt a swift, stinging dart of jealousy. "Edna?" she repeated.

He now made his way toward her. "Look how far out we are now."

"I can't. Who's Edna?"

"Well, it's complicated." He was teasing, his eyes dancing, but she was in no mood for it.

"One of the many other women you've slept with? What parish was she from?"

His eyes widened in astonishment. "Edna was an old school chum . . . of my grandmother's."

"You were teasing me, you deliberately misled me. Trying to make me think there's another woman in your life."

"Edna wants me to buy this," he continued, as if not hearing her. "It was her late husband's, and Lord knows she has no use for it. But of course she wants the world for it."

"You *were* leading me on, weren't you?"

He turned to her with a hurt, serious expression, which seemed completely out of place on the breezy, sunny deck of the boat. "What sort of man do you think I am? A promiscuous one? Amoral?"

"I don't know, Ellis." She paused. "You seem to know a lot about women."

"Of course I had lovers. Before seminary, before I became a priest. But none after I took the vows. None, till you."

"How was I to know?"

"Do you actually think there's another? Do you think I'd be unfaithful to you?"

She was unable to answer, taken aback by the melancholy tone in his voice.

"What sort of man do you think I am?" he demanded again, wounded, incredulous.

She sighed. "I'm sorry, Ellis." But she thought: How am I to know, when everything he gives me in the way of information comes in dribs and drabs and paltry crumbs, and I have to piece it all together like some infernal puzzle? She felt some sorrow over the serious turn their conversation had taken; the smile had fallen from his face.

"So, does Edna want much for her boat?"

He seemed relieved by the change in subject. "She

doesn't want money. She wants to barter for it. She sells antiques."

"Antiques?" Rose was not quite familiar with that idea.

"Old stuff. My house is filled with it, Rose. Hadn't you noticed?"

She had, but merely thought the furnishings were rather worn and sad, even decrepit; it never occurred to her they might be of any value. Ellis was now guiding the boat into a small calm inlet.

"You must have lots of things in the attic."

He seemed not to have heard. He gazed out over the water, shielding his eyes.

"This looks like a good place to drop anchor."

"What? Why?" She looked about in alarm. They were alone in the middle of the saucer-shaped inlet, the boat bobbing gently, waves lapping against the sides in a friendly sort of way. Still, she felt afraid: completely adrift, physically separated from the earth, only her and Ellis, who was now stripping off his clothes. He grinned at her. "You're not afraid to be alone out here with me, are you?" But he didn't wait for her answer and suddenly dived off the side of the boat. She shrieked.

"Ellis!"

She stared at the water frantically, looking for him, waiting for him to come up. "Ellis!" she continued to shout, terrified. She flailed at the water, splashing, vainly trying to find him. He emerged abruptly, laughing, his hair slicked back from his face, which seemed starker, the angles more pronounced in the harsh sunlight. He was laughing, reaching for her. She almost didn't recognize him.

"Come on in." He grabbed one of her arms. "Come, Rose. It's warmer here than in the sea."

She was stunned by how the smile, the laughter, transformed his face. "I . . . I can't swim."

"It's not deep. Look, I'm standing up." Only his head was

visible above the surface of the water; the rest of his body hovered ghostlike below. She didn't know whether to believe him or not. She shook her head resolutely, but suddenly he yanked her arm and pulled her in: She hit the water shrieking with outrage and dismay, but he was holding her so tightly, tighter than he'd ever embraced her before.

"I won't let you go," he was whispering to her, his voice mingling with the lapping waves. "I won't let you drown." Nevertheless, she actually struggled against him for a few moments out of mindless fear from the sudden shock of hitting the water. "Relax," he crooned in her ear. "Stop fighting. Rose? Rose, Rose . . ." Somehow that brought her around, hearing him repeat her name over and over, chanting it in her ear. She clung to him. "Ellis, you idiot," she murmured, chuckling softly, but embracing him now, clinging to him. Her initial panic spent, she felt oddly safe, secure, protected in the lukewarm waters, the soft waves and Ellis's powerful embrace; now she could feel the earth of the mucky bottom below with her big toe, the marine grasses teasing, twining about her legs. Against the sky and sea his eyes seemed an unbelievable, almost miraculous shade of blue. She had the magical sense of being enchanted, drawn into a spell. She hugged him tighter, drawing her legs up around him in an attempt to keep her own head above water.

8

"IT'S too bad herbal tea can't taste this good." Rose gave Lucas a wry smile, as she sipped from her paper Dunkin' Donuts cup. "I never used to be a coffee drinker, not till after the kids came, and I needed that extra jolt now and then." She grinned and took another gulp.

Lucas, who'd opted for plain, black tea, gazed at her in a serious way. "Theo gave me chamomile tea after I fell off a ladder and had a concussion. It really helped with the headaches. And then there was this—" He pulled up the sleeve of his sweater and showed Rose a pale, slightly freckled forearm. "I got a big scratch here, from a thorn bush, and it got all infected. Theo put some kind of poultice on it, some kind of big wet leaf, and it cleared right up."

Rose nodded. "Did Theo tell you there are harmful herbs as well as beneficial ones?"

"Oh, sure. There were actually poisonous plants in Theo's garden, plants we could never use. Theo said they were there for historical accuracy only."

"There would be no herb garden, if it weren't for me," she remarked in an offhand way. Lucas stared at her.

"I'm not bragging or boasting, or trying to take Ellis down a notch. But it's absolutely so. He had no interest in or knowledge of herbs, or gardening for that matter, before he met me. I'm just utterly intrigued that he took his life in that direction. But he's always had that interest in medicine. In drugs and potions and cures. And that preoccupation with his own health. He wasn't really a hypochondriac, but he was always very sensitive to pain of any kind. I remember the gossipy old housekeeper at St. Cyril's telling how she was always going out to get him this prescription or that, and that he made her buy five or six different brands of aspirin. When he was an ordinary priest, he'd go to the hospital on sick calls and explain to his parishioners all about their injuries or illnesses. Whether they wanted to know or not." She laughed. "But he'd also tell them what they could expect in the way of treatment, and he'd even argue with their doctors!"

"Was he ever a doctor? A medical student?"

"No. But his father was a physician. He ran a clinic for the poor in Portland, and when Ellis was off from school he had to accompany his father there. God knows what he must have witnessed as a child. But he learned an enormous amount as well."

"I'd forgotten that he was a diocesan priest," Lucas murmured, squirming a bit on the hard orange plastic seat. "I can't imagine him in that role at all. He's so quiet, private . . ."

"It was very hard for him. He wasn't happy—" She stopped herself, but Lucas leaned forward, intensely interested.

"Did something happen to him at that parish?"

"What? Oh, no, no. He was a splendid priest in his last parish. My parish. We didn't know what to make of him at first, he seemed so cool and distant. But he had this amazingly energetic streak: He was always out and about, making the calls the other priests didn't want to make. Visiting the sick, the prisoners, going out to highway accidents. He taught classes, the children's catechism, but also adult classes. Hearing confessions at any time of the day or night. And once, when an immigrant family turned up in town, he actually went door to door to find them a place to stay." Rose tilted her head, as if still marveling at this thirty years later. "He was conscientious and self-sacrificing, always giving up his time, always looking after others. . . . But always in his usual prickly manner." She shook her head, but was smiling ruefully. "He wasn't the friendliest priest you ever wanted to meet. Some days he seemed completely stone-cold, encased in ice."

Lucas nodded. "Yes, we saw that side of him often enough. But it wasn't . . ." He paused, frowning. "*Real*, somehow. It wasn't a deliberate or hurtful cold, more of an unintentional, accidental kind of coolness."

"That's true. He was born with that face, those expressions. Ellis really had no idea, no sense of his effect on people. I myself actually avoided him when he first came to our parish. I wouldn't go to his Masses and stayed away from him in the confessional—he was known for harsh penances! I was intimidated by him, unnerved . . . he was so different from any other priest I had ever known: a real patrician, you know, because he had that old-money blue-blood Protestant New England upbringing, and he carried himself like a man with breeding. Well, he'd graduated from Dartmouth, Ivy League and all that. Boarding school and a lineage that stretched back three hundred years. He came from wealth."

"Wow," Lucas murmured. "I had no idea."

"He taught the parish's adult education classes. The monsignor felt we needed to be schooled in our faith: Ha! All of us laborers and farmers and mill workers of Wisterville. I would go, every Thursday night, and sit way in the back. But gradually . . . I became impressed with him and less afraid of him; he was so intelligent, and a marvelous speaker despite . . . well, that odd shyness he had with people." And in her mind's eye a startling image came to her, one she could not quite share with Lucas. Ellis in his black cassock, his blond hair falling into his eyes, reading glasses at the end of his nose, his long, graceful arms gesturing as he spoke. She could barely remember the subject matter—Gnostics, Albigensians, Saint Jerome and Albertus Magnus and Bonaventure—it was all jumbled into a tangled, incomprehensible mess in her mind, but then she was not so much intrigued by the subject matter as by the speaker. Handsome Father Barlowe with his sweep of sandy hair and patrician profile and quirky Maine accent talking of *Gahd, the Fah-thah*, his voice rising and swaying, trembling with enthusiasm when he stumbled—seemingly by accident—onto something that particularly interested or intrigued him, the faintest pink blush spreading across his cheekbones. . . .

She blinked: Back in the glaring pink-and-orange donut shop on the edge of a remote Pennsylvania highway at 10 P.M., sitting across from a somber, rumpled young man who gaped at her with an inexplicable sort of hunger and curiosity.

"Do you want another donut?" she asked him. He shook his head.

"No, no. Go on with your story."

"It's boring," she said, teasing him.

"Please."

"One night, Ellis was talking . . . and it became very clear that he was in tremendous discomfort. He was pale, his voice barely audible, and he kept clutching his head. I remember sitting there, watching him, understanding what was wrong. He had some kind of monstrous headache, and he was fighting it, struggling to get around it somehow, struggling to finish his talk. He managed to speak for about twenty minutes, then dismissed us all with a feeble wave of his hand before sinking down onto a bench, clutching his head in his hands."

"It was a migraine," Lucas offered excitedly, "one of his migraines. Gosh, when Theo had one of those, you knew you had to stay away from him."

"Now I'll tell you a little about myself at that time," Rose continued, draining the rest of her coffee. "I was the town nurserywoman. I'd inherited the business from my first husband, who sold only foundation shrubs and Christmas trees, but after he died I diversified a bit and brought in flowers and house plants and some other exotic plants. Herbs were a bit unusual to plant back in the early sixties; they didn't really catch on till the hippies came along, but I started growing and selling them on my own. I remembered the old nuns from my childhood, telling me about this cure or that one, and I began experimenting, dabbling in herbal cures myself—I guess I was ahead of my time!" She laughed. "I came up with a few mild remedies for ordinary complaints; I made up bags of tea that I would sell at my shop. I actually developed something of a following, though all the townspeople considered me, well, a bit eccentric. But folks would drive up from New Haven or Hartford for my special tea.

"When I saw Ellis sitting there, in pain, I knew I had to at least offer to help him. So I walked toward him— It's funny, isn't it, how one moment, one small action, can change your life forever? If I hadn't approached Ellis that day, I might never have approached him at all, and he would have left, maybe to go to another parish or to the monastery and I never would have met Burt. I never would have had my children and grandchildren or the incredible, full life I've had these past thirty years. You know, I think we should order some more coffee, or they might throw us out of here."

Lucas said nothing. He simply stared at her, resting his chin in his hands, transfixed.

"I went up to Ellis and said, 'I have something for that headache, Father, something that works when nothing else does.' Well, he glanced up at me with a look of utter and complete skepticism." In fact, she remembered, there was something angry, even malevolent, in that look he shot up at her, as if he suspected her of trying to fool or trick him. Did he know of her reputation as a slightly loony gardener and shopkeeper, the town's eccentric young widow? Dressed deliberately in obstinately plain clothes, shapeless dresses and sweaters, her long, pre-hippie hair in a braid down her back, lips without lipstick, eyes adorned only by the creases and crinkles the sun had given her?

And yet, he rose and went with her, allowing her to lead him out into the street and down a few blocks toward the outskirts of the village, where her small farm and farmhouse lay. She remembered the proud sort of giddiness she felt walking beside him in the dark, as if she were bringing home some special sort of prize, but aware, too, of his terrible pain, which made him rigid and silent, moving with great slowness.

"So I brought him to my house and brewed him a cup of this special headache tea. Actually,"—Rose laughed out loud, a great delighted laugh that filled the donut shop, startling the rather bored employees behind the counter— "it was the tea I brewed for my own *menstrual* problems! But I thought there were enough calming and pain-killing elements in it to help his headaches."

Drink it down, Father Barlowe. It'll help.

His face contorting. Pale, in the muted light of her kitchen. A single lamp glowing; his long, slender, somewhat bony fingers wrapped tightly around one of her blue-and-white cups, which was filled with a clear, amber liquid. A timid sort of sip.

Oh, Rose. This is awful.

I'm sorry. . . . The willow bark and the other herbs give it a strange flavor, but . . . it should help.

If you say so. An odd, amused look at her, as if they were sharing a joke. Sharing an embarrassing secret. Was that the beginning of their bond, that complicity? He drained his cup, then sat waiting, as if for an instantaneous effect.

You should go now, Father, and rest. Go back, and go to sleep.

"The next week, at the Thursday-night lecture, he said nothing to me. He did not even acknowledge my presence, and I was fuming. I felt humiliated! If it hadn't worked, the least he could have done was *told* me. But a few nights later, he showed up at my door. Again, in excruciating pain. But so humble, contrite . . ."

Please, Rose, if you could . . .

I didn't think it worked for you. Her own voice, sharp, wounded. *You never even said . . .*

It did help, a little. I think it did. I need to try it again. Oh, Rose, you can't imagine what this pain is like. Nothing helps it, not aspirin, not prescription drugs.

And, of course, she'd softened, forgetting her own annoyance at him, her own hurt. *Where does it hurt?* she asked, her fingers darting out to touch his forehead. *Here?* He placed his own hand over hers and guided it, pressed it over his left eye, a soft, faint moan escaping his lips. His skin was warm, almost burning to the touch. . . .

"So you're the one who developed the special tea he drinks when he gets his headaches?" Lucas asked. "You mean, it's actually a *menstrual* remedy? That's . . . that's pretty funny. Did you ever tell him?"

"No, I didn't. Because it worked for him. I'm sure a lot

of it is power of suggestion, a mental sort of thing. But Ellis came back again and again. Until about six months later, when he left our parish."

"That's when he went out to Benedetto?"

"No. He left the priesthood, Lucas. He walked out and just left. Or fled. He went to his home in Maine. To a house he had inherited from his father."

Lucas stared at her, crestfallen.

"It's true," she said, softly, sympathetically. "*That's* how Ellis deals with things, by running away. Escaping. He means no harm by it, he thinks he's doing everyone a favor. Sparing everyone from his moods, from his own kind of madness. But he never seems aware that the hurt and pain he leaves behind is worse than whatever we have to put up with from him."

"So that's why you think he's run away now."

"I can't help but think that."

"Rose, we have to find him. I just have to know what's happened to him."

"Speaking of running away . . ."

"I know, I know. But I can't go back to Benedetto until I know that he's safe, or at peace with himself."

Rose studied him for a long time. He certainly could not accompany her to Maine: She needed to make that journey alone. And yet she suspected that Lucas, like baby ducks or deer raised in captivity, was not quite ready to be set free in the world. A few days on the farm, she thought, might help him make the transition.

"Well, we're not getting anywhere sitting here. Come on, we have a long drive ahead of us, a long night. And New York City to get through."

"I can drive," he volunteered, eagerly.

"It'll be another five hours, at least, to Connecticut." And many more, she thought wearily, till I reach Maine.

9

B Y late June, the herbs Rose had planted in the "pharmacy" garden, the bed of plants nestled against the curving porch, had burst upward and outward in feathery mounds and voluptuous spikes. The basil and lavender erupted into flower, and the slightest breeze sent their aromas wafting across the porch and in through the windows of the house.

She watched as Ellis hunted for ravenous slugs and snails in the garden by flashlight after dark: The beam of light illuminated his pale hand as it swept over the plants, searching, caressing, stroking each leaf. She waited up on the porch for him to come to her next. When he kissed her, there would still be the lingering scent of mint, of camphor, of thyme or of anise in his clothes, on the tips of his fingers.

But there was no scent of tobacco or stale cigarette smoke: At her urging, he somehow managed to quit smoking altogether, giving it up cold turkey, all in one day. He was peevish and irritable for days afterward, but Rose was pleased to see him rid of that addiction. Now, she thought, if she could just get rid of the medicines that clogged their cabinet in the bathroom: old prescriptions, analgesics, aspirin stockpiled as if he expected some medical catastrophe to hit, a tidal wave of illness. She never saw him take any of this medicine, save the aspirin, which he gulped by the handful when his migraines came on.

Their lovemaking, she thought, had begun to lose some of its intensity and insistence. Fueled no longer by neediness or desperation, Ellis seemed more at ease with her in bed, more affectionate. He would play with her hair, or tickle and tease, and during the act itself would murmur her name in an incantatory way. Afterward, he would not fall immediately into sleep, as if drugged, but would nestle against her, chatting aimlessly, usually about the garden or the weather, or some passage in the Durant that had captured his interest.

She thought she saw a new, mellower Ellis emerging, but he still could, without warning, descend into coldness and silence, retreating behind some wall where she could not reach him. At such times she wondered how she could love such a man. How could she stay with him? Was it something lacking in herself, or perhaps a surfeit of empathy or pity? Perhaps, she thought, it was merely a sort of sexual fetish, of needing a deeply needy man. For that was how she saw him: a man unable to give words to his need—for love, for compassion—or to even admit to it. In any case, she was not ready to leave Ellis just yet, though she understood that this was the only real conclusion to their relationship. She knew she could not cure his spirit or heal the holes in his heart and soul; eventually such holes would tear into her as well. She was only beginning to realize his problems were not necessarily centered on his lost vocation, the spiritual life he had abandoned, but that they stretched further back, deeper into his past, and were perhaps rooted in his boyhood.

But for now, there was the magnificent sex: no small gift for a plain woman on the edge of middle age, who might never—she believed—know such exquisite pleasure again with a man. And there was the distraction of the garden, the sea and the strange but splendid house itself, with its locked, boarded-up rooms upstairs still beckoning to her, inviting her to come and explore.

At Keating's Nursery and Pick-Ur-Own, Rose emerged from her truck warily, clutching her own empty quart baskets. She wanted strawberries—Ellis loved them, but they had not attempted to grow them in the garden. Too risky, she'd thought. She hoped to avoid Burt Keating; he had accosted her on her last visit: "Missus Barlowe! How're things going on the old estate?" But no sooner had she begun to make her way out into one of the more distant fields, when he suddenly materialized—a scarecrowlike figure, lanky, bony, with comically red hair and weathered face—shouting with delighted recognition: "Hey, Missus Barlowe!"

She jumped. A few other customers turned to eye her curiously. Before she could say anything more, he took her by the arm and ushered her into what seemed to be a small retail shop located inside a barn.

"Got some irises, all potted up, but I want to show you something first. Look at these gladiolies. Gorgeous, huh? My brother does them, grows 'em right here in the greenhouse. Here he is now. Hey, Graham."

Graham was as red-haired as his older brother, but

smaller, thinner, balding, his face an odd triangular shape, a wispy beard coating his chin.

"It's Barlowe's wife. I told you, he came back with a bride, of all things."

"I'm not Barlowe's wife," she murmured, abashed. "I'm . . . I'm just the groundskeeper, really." She didn't feel the brothers needed to know the true nature of her relationship with Ellis. Graham turned to his brother with a smug, self-satisfied expression.

"Told you," he said drily to Burt, who flushed in confusion.

"I'm sorry, uh, Miss—"

"Connolly. Mrs. Connolly. But you can call me Rose."

"Graham said you two couldn't be married. I didn't believe him, though. You just seemed like such a classy lady. Someone a Barlowe would marry."

"Burt, shut up," Graham snapped. He had a whiny, high-pitched voice, a contemptuous manner that made her wince and bristle. He turned his gaze to Rose. "I used to know Ellis," he said in a challenging voice. "A while ago. When we were boys together."

"Actually, we never had much to do with them," Burt injected cheerfully. "Those Barlowes. Wrong side of the family."

"You're related to Ellis?"

"Oh, sure. Everyone here on the island is, in some way or other. Everyone in Wainscott comes from Barlowe blood. Our grandma was a Barlowe. The old parson's sister."

"The old parson?"

"You know, your fellow's grandpa."

She squinted at Burt for a moment, looking for some family resemblance. He was long and tall and lanky like Ellis, but that was about it: garden grime hid most of his features, which were irregular, reddened and chapped. But he did have amazing eyes, bright, almost turquoise blue.

"You're . . . cousins, then," she murmured.

"I guess. But we never much bothered with them. They kind of turned their backs on our grandma, 'cause she married down."

"Ellis's grandfather . . . was a minister?" she murmured, wonderingly. "And his father was a physician, is that right?"

Both men fell silent. Graham ventured a look at his brother, then gave her what clearly seemed a sly, troublemaker's smile.

"Yes, the doctor. The *unfortunate* Dr. Barlowe."

On the way back, she took the long way around the island, stopping in town so she could duck into the meeting hall of the Congregational Church. She made her way down the cool, mint-green halls, feeling vaguely at home, studying the portraits of parsons that lined the walls. The first was a seventeenth-century gentleman with flowing white locks named Elias Barlowe. Several generations later, another Elias, and finally she paused before the somber portrait of an elderly gentleman dressed in black, clutching a Bible. A long, bony, frowning face, slate-blue eyes, bristly gray crew cut. *Rev. Ellis Barlowe, 1854–1953*, read the inscription beneath.

"Don't let old pastor Barlowe scare you," an older woman passing by remarked cheerfully. "He's gone now, but he was much more daunting in real life, let me tell you."

Rose leaned forward, squinting at the painting: The man did not much resemble Ellis, but she thought she saw some similarity in the leanness of his frame, the cut of his jaw. Certainly in his eyes.

"A grim crusty old man, one of the old fire-and-brimstone preachers, if you know what I mean."

"Interesting," Rose murmured, backing her way out of the hall. "Did you know," she heard one woman say to another, sotto voce, as she left the hall, "that old Barlowe place is occupied again?"

After dinner that evening, Rose brought out the straw-berries she'd picked at the Keatings' farm. Ellis was pleased.

"Where did you get these? They're magnificent!"

"I picked them."

"You're kidding. Are they wild?"

"Of course not. I picked them at your cousins' farm."

His face froze, then crinkled into a distinctly fearful look. "Which cousins?"

"The Keatings? Burt and Graham?"

"Why did you go *there*?" His voice was measured, calm, but she sensed an acid disapproval behind it, which baffled her.

"You don't . . . like them?"

"Why did you go there?" he demanded.

"That's where we ordered the shrubs from. They're the only farm on the island, in the area. Where should I have gone?"

"I don't want to do business with them anymore."

"Why not?" She bit her lip, afraid to pry and risk his anger. But her curiosity was overwhelming her.

He folded his arms together, fixing her with a cool gaze. "What did they say about me?"

"Only . . . that you were . . . related. What's wrong with them? What happened between you?"

He pointed to the odd little ridge, the bump or break, at the bridge of his nose.

"They . . . beat you?"

"This was a gift from my dear cousins, the Keatings. Dis-figured for life by those shits."

"Why?"

He shrugged.

"You had a fight with them?"

"They were just stupid farm thugs, and I was the rich sissy cousin. Isn't that reason enough? There have always been such demons in my life, Rose, bullies who hated me for God knows what reason. There were boys at school, and when I came home in the summer, the Keatings, lying in wait for me. As if I didn't have enough trouble, just dealing with Dad—" He stopped now, clearly annoyed with himself for rambling on. "Just don't . . . don't bother with them anymore, Rose. Please."

She went to the stove to put on the tea water. Ellis's darkening mood presaged another headache. She thought about the way he spoke that word: *Dad*. With a mixture of exasperation and nostalgia, too, a hint of yearning. But that was one of the taboo subjects, something not to be pursued just yet. Certainly not this minute.

"I saw your grandfather today," she ventured. "A picture of him." He stared at her blankly for a moment, then a worried expression crept into his face.

"The old Reverend, huh?" He shivered in a comical way, then chuckled softly, as if they were sharing a joke.

"You have the same color eyes."

"That's all we had in common."

"How did you end up . . . a Catholic?"

He moved away from her, back toward the table. "That was my mother's faith." He turned, his face calm, benign. "She was French-Canadian."

"Oh? What was she like?"

"I don't remember." His voice was soft, untroubled.

"Did she die when you were young?"

"What were you doing down at the Congregational Church?"

"Ellis!" she snapped, snatching at the bubbling, hissing tea kettle. She yelped as boiling water shot out at her hand and dropped the kettle back onto the stove. "I was asking about your mother, why did you change the subject?

Ouch . . ." Mindlessly, she stuck her seared hand into her mouth, as if trying to suck the pain out of it. Ellis gently pulled her hand away.

"Get me some butter," she whimpered.

"No, no. You need some ice. Putting grease on it will only seal in the heat and slow down the healing process." He opened the freezer and took out a tray of ice. He wrapped some of it in a dishcloth and gently, tenderly dabbed it against her reddened skin. She smiled, weakly.

"You seem to know something about first aid. Were you a Boy Scout?"

"I have some medical training, you know. More for shrapnel and blown-off limbs, nothing we're likely to encounter here, I hope."

Puzzled, she cocked her head. "Not . . . Korea?"

"What did you think I did during the Second World War? Did you think I was a draft dodger?"

"You're full of surprises," she murmured. "I don't think that I could ever completely figure you out."

"I was at Dartmouth for most of the war, but I enlisted right after graduation. I was stationed on an army hospital ship in the Mediterranean, then at a hospital in Algeria. It was," he smiled in a wan way, still clutching her hand, gingerly lifting and lowering the ice on her burn, "one of the happier times in my life."

"*Happy?* You must have seen some terrible things."

He shrugged. "Blood, gore, dismembered bodies? Oh sure. That stuff doesn't bother me. Or it didn't bother me, after a while. It becomes a job, and yet . . . for once, it was a job with people that I was good at. I never before felt so completely necessary. Needed. It was a feeling I'd never quite had before, certainly not growing up here. And, of course, I was caught up in *history*, in the tremendous drama of the war. It was very exciting, it was very . . . fulfilling." He talked in a flushed, animated way. She'd never seen him like this before. She stared at him in wonderment. "In a way," he continued, "it led me into the priesthood. I saw that I was fit for a life of discipline, of service, but I didn't want to stay in the army. Or become a doctor. I'd actually begun thinking about the seminary while I was over there; it seemed a natural sort of progression. Of course, there was the whole connection with my mother, too . . ."

"What connection?"

He rose. "I'm going to put some gauze on this to let it breathe." The confessional tone had fallen away, replaced by the brisk, assuring tone of the doctor, the healer. "I don't think it's a very bad burn at all."

10

SHORTLY after dawn, Rose and Lucas arrived at the gates
of her farm and nursery business in the rolling Connecticut countryside northeast of Hartford. Lucas, bleary-
eyed from long hours of staring at the road, his back stiff,
unaccustomed to the task of driving, gaped at Rose's spread:
rows of greenhouses, a large barn that functioned as a retail
center and acres upon acres of plants, young trees, flowers,
corn, rambling pumpkin vines and other vegetables.

"It's huge," he mumbled. "Bigger than the abbey. How
do you keep track of it all?"

"We manage." Rose jumped out of her truck and surveyed the place in a pleased sort of way, one hand on her
hip. Despite the earliness of the hour, the place was buzzing
with activity: Lucas saw laborers digging in the fields and
landscapers pulling their trucks in, trying to get a jump on
the day. Like the monastery, he thought, a farm business
gets under way swift and early.

A short, wiry fellow of about twenty or twenty-five was

quickly loping in their direction. He had the firm, muscled body of a man, but his face was round and childishly plump. He broke into a grin when he saw Rose.

"Momma!" He hugged her tightly, nearly lifting her off the ground. Rose chuckled and squeezed him, running her fingers through his coppery hair, rubbing his soft, freckled cheeks.

"My baby, Tommy." Tommy beamed at Lucas; his dark blue eyes were curious, alert.

"Don't go away again, Mom." He pleaded. "Mandy was mean."

"I wish I could tell you I'm not," she said with a sigh. "But we'll talk about it, Tommy boy. Look, here's my other baby."

Another man, somewhat taller, more serious, with Rose's tapestry-hazel eyes and darker hair, was walking toward her swiftly; two small red-haired girls danced behind him. Hank, thought Lucas. This son gave Rose a quick, cool peck on the cheek. "Mom," he murmured, while his girls wrapped themselves around Rose's legs.

"Grandma! Did you *get* us anything?"

"It wasn't that kind of trip, darlings. Tommy, go and fetch my overnight bag from the car. I have to repack it. Girls, let me go. I have to talk to Aunt Mandy now—"

"Mom, wait—" Hank laid a hand on her shoulder, frowning. Rose glanced at him nervously, her eyes questioning him. Hank's eyes turned suddenly, in a confused way, to Lucas.

"This is Lucas, one of the monks from that monastery I visited," Rose explained. "He had family out this way, so he hitched a ride with me. Helped with the driving."

Hank nodded, in a curt greeting. Rose grabbed his arm. "Hank, what's wrong?"

"It's Dad. He's . . . in the hospital."

"*No!*"

"I know you don't want him there. He had that breathing thing again, and Mandy freaked. She had an ambulance bring him in."

"Oh, good Lord!" Rose seemed thoroughly exasperated. "So I suppose he's hooked up to that whole contraption now, machines, tubes—"

"Yes, Mom. It's really serious this time. He's on life support, a respirator."

"He wanted to die at *home*. You *knew* that."

"Yeah, but nobody has anything on paper. No living will, or whatever you call it."

"Why did Mandy do that? I told her—"

"Mom, listen. It's one thing for you to sit here and just let Dad choke and die. It's not in Mandy, or me, to be able to do that." He addressed her sternly and with vague disgust. Rose obviously sensed this and stalked away from him into the house. Lucas was left behind, feeling awkward, with taciturn Hank, who jammed his hands into his pockets in a gesture of resignation or annoyance.

"This is some place your mom has," Lucas offered, feebly. Hank frowned at him.

"You got family near here?"

"Uh . . . sort of."

"They in farming?"

"No, they're all lawyers."

Hank thought about this for a moment and ambled off, perhaps in search of his daughters. Tommy amiably brushed by Lucas on the front porch, and Lucas followed him into the house, walking in the direction of arguing female voices.

"What could I do? It was *impossible*, Mom, an impossible situation!"

"You knew what he wanted, what we agreed on—"

"You and Dad agreed on it, but *you* weren't here! You took off, to some crazy place I couldn't even contact you at—"

"Oh come on, Amanda, I couldn't have foreseen this! I cannot put my whole life on hold, waiting, waiting. I have to live, too!" Lucas saw Rose addressing a tall, blond woman whose back was to him: a woman he knew, from talking with Rose, to be nearly thirty, yet she had the stance, the demeanor, the taut, slim body—encased in snug jeans and T-shirt—of a teenager. "Like I don't," she retorted, bitterly. "I put my life on hold so you can run off on some goose chase to Ohio or wherever, and now you're screaming at me because I took my father to the hospital, because I saved his life!"

"We should not be arguing about this. It's not . . . It's not going to matter, because . . . Burt is going to die now, no matter what. I suppose it really isn't important where, anymore." She reached out for her daughter with both arms, but Amanda did not want to be comforted. She turned away from her mother. And Lucas gasped, audibly.

Amanda stared at him, her hands on her hips. "Who's that?" she demanded, somewhat contemptuously. Lucas continued to stare at her, at her angular face and long, straight nose, those gray-blue icy eyes, even the scornful, impatient expression . . . *Theo!* he thought, in utter shock.

"This is Lucas Reardon." Rose now placed an arm about his shoulder, obviously feeling the need to lay her hands on someone. "He's from the abbey I visited, and he helped me drive home."

"Why?"

"Because he has family here, too. Mandy, make us some coffee."

"Mom, really! When was the last time you slept?"

Rose blinked. "Slept? Oh, I don't know. It's been a long trip. And I was in a hurry to get home."

"You hardly need coffee," Amanda snapped. She turned her gaze to Lucas. It was the same unnervingly direct look Theo would focus on him when he needed to know some unpleasant or unexpected fact or truth. "And you, when did you sleep last?"

"I don't recall. In my cell, at Benedetto." God, it seemed like centuries ago, he thought.

Rose led him firmly to a small room at the end of the hallway. "This is your room for now. Go sleep for a day or so, then call your parents. You'll feel braver when you have a clear head."

He sank obediently onto the bed, fully clothed, Amanda's and Rose's voices still rang in his ears—Amanda's face was firmly planted in his brain—as he drifted off to sleep.

Rose returned to the kitchen to confront Amanda. Her prickly up-and-down daughter seemed to veer from one crisis to another. Bad lovers, jobs gone awry, even one bad marriage behind her and an abortion Rose wasn't supposed to know about. At nearly thirty, Amanda seemed not to have outgrown the rebelliousness and contemptuous attitude she'd developed as a teenager. Rose wished passionately that her daughter would marry again and have children of her own. That would straighten her out, thought Rose. *It certainly straightened me out. And in a hurry, too.*

"So," Amanda drawled, when Rose walked back into the kitchen. "Didn't you find him?"

Rose shook her head, defeated.

"Gone, huh?"

"I have to find him, Mandy."

"While Dad lies dying in his hospital bed."

"Well, if he's on life support, there's no real danger of his dying anytime soon, is there?"

"You do blame me, for all that."

"No, no, Amanda. I'm just telling you, I have one more trip to make. I *have* to make it, and I will make it. Your father would understand perfectly. He knows, he remembers what Ellis was like, he would approve, Mandy. Don't roll your eyes at me. I know your father much better than you do."

"I don't believe it. You're actually going to take off again? *Now?*"

"Your father is not going anywhere. A few days isn't going to make any difference. When I return, we'll talk with the doctors and decide what step to take next."

"Like whether to pull the plug? How very convenient, Mother. We'll just postpone Dad's death while you go traipsing off in search of your long-lost lover."

"It isn't like that, it's far more complicated than you realize. I think Ellis may be in mortal danger, too."

Amanda folded her arms together: a sullen, disapproving child.

"Did you ever love him?" she asked. Rose cocked her head.

"Who?"

"My father!"

"I loved him very much."

"No, I mean my *father*, Burt Keating."

"You know I do. With Ellis, it was a different kind of love." She searched her daughter's face. "Haven't you the least bit of curiosity about him, Mandy?"

"No. *No.* He wasn't my father. Just the guy with the sperm. Burt was my father, nothing changes that." Amanda sank into a chair, exasperated. "I'm not judging you, Mom. I think I understand, I really do. But you have to see the timing of this . . . it's rotten! How can you leave Dad now, of all times?"

"Because . . . because . . . your dad is . . . *safe*, now. I know that's a funny way of putting it. But he's in there, with all those doctors and nurses and all that technology;

it's like he's in a different country now, and he's being cared for and looked after and there is nothing we can do for him anymore. I know where he is, where he'll be, when I return, but no one knows where Ellis is. I'm certain he's in some kind of trouble or distress, and I think I'm the only one who can help him."

"Then why didn't he come to you first?"

"I don't know, Amanda. That hurts me, very much, but it also tells me how troubled he must be. I'm pretty sure where he went, and if I don't go up there and check it out, now, today, it'll haunt me for the rest of my life."

"Is this some kind of late mid-life crisis? Is this what I have to look forward to?"

"Don't be flip," Rose snapped, angry now. "You have absolutely no idea what this means to me. I don't even want to discuss it with you anymore. Obviously, you've never loved anyone properly or passionately enough to understand—"

"Obviously, I haven't," Amanda murmured, seemingly wounded and chastened at the same time. Rose's face crumpled.

"Mandy, sweetheart, I'm sorry. I shouldn't have—"

"Enough, Mom. You're overwrought. A classic example of sleep deprivation. Go to bed."

"I should go over and see your father—"

"No, you need to sleep first. I won't let you go to the hospital in this condition; they might admit you as a patient. And I want you to be in a better mood when you see Dad."

Rose laid a hand on her shoulder. This time Amanda did not flinch or move away. "All right. Wake me up in a few hours though, okay? Don't let me sleep past noon."

"Don't worry. Good ol' Mandy will hold down the fort. It's not like I have anything else to do."

"You're doing a good job at the shop."

"Mom, I *hate* it. I am so sick of plants and bushes and fresh vegetables, I could scream."

Rose sighed: the old refrain. Over and over again, and yet Amanda seemed unwilling, or unable, to do anything else.

"Listen, that boy I brought back with me is a runaway from the monastery. He has to call his family, or at least his abbot. I cannot take him with me to Maine. Just see that he calls someone. Give him some money, if you have to, and send him away."

"Thanks a lot. Just what I need, another body to be responsible for. Oh, don't worry, Mom. I'll see that he gets taken care of."

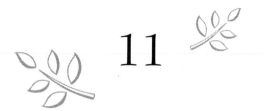

11

EDNA, the antiques dealer, stood on the front porch in a tweed suit, sunglasses and straw hat, leaning on a gnarled-wood cane. Ellis groaned when he saw her.

"And good day to you, too, Barlowe. Might I come in?"

"You might not," he snapped.

"Why so testy this morning, my boy?"

"Look, I found a dealer in Portland, far more astute than you, dear lady, in determining the worth of my heirlooms."

"That's a pity, Barlowe, because I have a customer who's *very* interested in some items you have here." She hobbled into the house, brushing roughly past Rose. "A very avid collector, as it happens, of antiquarian books."

"I have no books for sale."

"Oh, come. You think I'm senile? You think I forgot that collection of your father's? And him, in my shop, every month, asking for more. What happened to all those books, Barlowe? There must have been thousands. What did you do with them all when your father died?"

"I have no idea what Grandfather did with them," Ellis replied blandly. "They're probably all in the library of the Wainscott Congregational Church."

"They're not," Edna snapped. "You could make a small fortune off those books, if you bothered to find them. The collector's a doctor, like your father, particularly interested in medical subjects."

"Sorry, Edna. Nothing else is for sale at this time." He steered her to the door and locked it behind her. Then he leaned up against it wearily, his eyes closed.

"What kind of a man was your father?" Rose asked, softly.

For a moment, he did not answer. He opened his eyes and gave her a long, severe look. "I don't know what you've heard," he said in a low, barely audible voice. "In town, from the neighbors, whoever. It's gossip, filthy rumor. None of it's *true*, Rose."

"I hadn't heard anything," she whispered.

"He was a good man," he continued. "A decent man. He ran a clinic for the poor in Portland. He charged nothing for his services and never turned anyone away."

"How remarkable."

"Oh yes, very remarkable. Because he was an *atheist*, you see. He had no belief, whatsoever, in a merciful God, no use for organized religion in any shape or form." He began to pace, his hands reaching for his pockets, as if for his long-discarded cigarettes. "I was actually forbidden to attend church, even my grandfather's church. My spiritual education was replaced with a more, well, pragmatic sort of apprenticeship. He used to bring me with him. To the clinic, on his house calls. He wanted me to see, firsthand, the full range of human misery, of pain, of suffering. He gave me little time to be spoiled, Rose." He sighed, and his gaze turned upward, toward the paneled ceiling. "It's incredible, but sometimes I feel his presence here still, so strongly."

And then, in a small, querulous voice: "I should never have come back here. But where else could I go?"

Rose was astonished at the strange longing, the regret she heard in his voice.

"It sounds as if you . . . miss him. Did you love him?"

He grimaced. "I don't want to talk about him anymore."

"He hurt you? He was bad to you?"

"Oh, I was just never good enough for him. Never smart enough, sharp enough, strong enough. I never did anything right, as far as he was concerned. And I've proved him right, it seems." His eyes moved upward. "I was supposed to be a doctor, too. I couldn't do it, I just couldn't. . . . And the thing I did choose, I failed at."

Rose took in a deep breath: This was the first real admission he'd made about his vocation.

"He's laughing at me, Rose, I'm sure of it. He's still here, just howling at the absurdity of it all."

"You don't actually believe in ghosts, do you?"

"I do believe," he said, in a quiet, dead-certain voice, "that the dead do come back to haunt and torment the living. Not as shadowy apparitions or walking corpses. But in more subtle ways."

"I didn't think you believed in anything anymore."

He looked at her in a startled way. "You don't really know me that well, yet."

She waited, patiently, until he took his solitary walk that evening—still agitated, edgy, troubled, she thought, by memories of his father—then crept upstairs with a claw hammer. She began removing nails from the boarded-over door, one by one, mindful she was doing something she shouldn't, something that might offend or enrage Ellis. Inviting the troubled spirits downstairs. But she couldn't stop.

It was a surprisingly easy task; the nails came out cleanly, without rust, as if they had been hammered in only recently. She removed the middle two boards and was able to squeeze through this space into the second floor.

She wandered down a long hallway lined with bedrooms. As she'd uneasily suspected, there was absolutely no evidence of bat or rodent trouble; the only pests Ellis wanted to seal off were ghosts or memories. The hall was lined with a rich Oriental runner, 1890s wallpaper in pristine condition, framed lithographs covered in a gossamer coat of dust on the wall. The rooms were all small, but exquisitely, even lavishly, furnished with antiques like those Rose had seen in museums, the Atheneum in Hartford. On the walls she found a few sepia-toned photographs framed in tarnished silver. A photo of a somber, fair-haired boy in a sailor suit, sitting on the house's front steps. Ellis: She recognized the eyes, the shape of his face and chin, the mournful downward slant of his mouth.

At the end of the hallway was a set of sliding doors: She tried to open these, but they were locked. She knelt and tried to look in through the keyhole and the slit between the doors. She caught just a glimpse of what seemed to be a magnificent room: bookcases, fireplace, Oriental rugs, wood paneling—a flash of light. Then she remembered: the balcony.

She made her way back down the hall, taking care to replace the boards and nails, then went downstairs and out of the house, to the barn. She gazed up into the rafters, certain she'd seen a ladder in there, somewhere. She finally located it—worn gray wood, sticky with spiderwebs—pinned against the back wall by old fence posts and bamboo rakes.

You are one crazy woman, she told herself. She tugged at the ladder and somehow managed to free it from the other debris. She was holding it up straight, trying to gauge its strength, when she saw Ellis standing at the barn door, silhouetted against the waning sun. She couldn't see his face or make out the expression on it, but what she saw in the stiffness of his stance chilled her.

"What are you doing with that ladder?" His tone was both melancholy and angry, the tone of a priest confronting a persistent sinner.

"Thought I'd go after those bats," she said, calmly. "In your attic."

"Were you actually going to climb up there—" Incredulous, he yanked the ladder out of her hands and threw it to the floor, where it fell with a great clatter. "Couldn't you have asked me, first? Have you taken to sneaking around behind my back?"

"Why are you shouting at me? What have I done that's so awful?"

"What is this *sick* obsession you have with my upstairs?"

"It's not sick. It's just curiosity. Ellis, what's wrong with you?"

"Simple curiosity? That's what drove you to the Keatings, is it? You won't trust me, you won't believe me. You have to dig, dig, dig constantly into my worthless past! What *is* it, Rose? What do you need so desperately to know? There's nothing, do you understand? Nothing!"

He stalked off from her. This time she followed him back to the house, but when she began to mount the steps, he suddenly wheeled around, his face still contorted with anger.

"Get *out!*" he shouted. "Just get the hell out of here!"

She stared at him, her mouth dropping open.

"Go away, I said." He suddenly shoved her backward, and she managed to catch the banister to keep herself from falling.

"Can't I . . . can't I even get my things?"

"No." His voice was raw from shouting now. "I don't need you here, I don't want you. Get out!"

She turned and ran to her truck. The keys happened to be in the ignition, so she turned them, started the truck up and roared out of the driveway in a state of panic and confusion.

The first place she came to was Keating's Nursery, which was closed for the evening. It was mercifully empty, deserted, so she pulled into the parking lot, turned off the truck and sat there until dusk, hugging herself. Shivering, she wondered what in the world she would do next.

She was at a complete loss: Who was at fault here? Was he being irrational, or actually trying to hide something from her? "But nothing was up there," she murmured aloud. "Nothing but nice furniture, old photographs . . ." Had she missed something, something so damning or humiliating that he feared it would repulse her, drive her away?

Or is it *me*, she wondered: snooping, sneaking about, searching for . . . what? Clues? Answers to questions she couldn't ask? He'd clearly regarded her curiosity as suspicion, doubt, mistrust.

Wasn't it?

"I don't know," she whispered into the darkness. "I just don't know." She did have that same vague, sickening sense she'd felt, in the beginning, with her husband, of something being amiss, something starting to veer out of place or go wrong.

Wait till night, she thought. Wait till he's asleep, creep in and get my things. Then leave. Oh, Rose, you are no judge of men. She felt too miserable, too despondent to cry. She rubbed her arms and stared out at the sunset and the Keatings' fields, which stretched toward the sea. There was a small shack silhouetted against the sky—a boathouse? Smoke house?

"Miss . . . Missus Connolly?" Suddenly there was Burt Keating right beside her, at her window. She glanced up at him in alarm. "You okay?" he asked, his brow deeply furrowed with concern.

"I'm . . . I'm fine."

"We're closed now."

"I know. I'm sorry. I needed to pull off the road for a moment, and this seemed a good spot. A good spot to watch the sunset."

"Where was you going?"

She struggled to come up with some valid destination, some reason to be out. She couldn't. "The truth is, Mr. Barlowe is in a terrible mood. I just needed to get away for a bit."

"Ah." He nodded, as if understanding perfectly.

"I guess I should be leaving."

"I could make you a cup of tea. Or something. You look chilled."

"No, no," she protested, but thought: Where else do I have to go? What will I do? "I don't want to put you out."

A sly sort of smile crossed his lips. "You ain't putting me out at all. Not at all."

"I used to run a small nursery myself," she told him, holding the warm tea in her hands. They were sitting in the darkened office of his retail shop; a lit candle was quaintly flickering in the dark. He made tea the way she liked it best: almost black, bitingly strong, bracing. "It was down in Connecticut."

He snickered. "And you came up here to garden? All this salt and wind—"

"I know," she murmured. "Crazy, isn't it?"

"Why'd you come?"

"Because Ellis asked me to."

Burt stared down at his own mug of tea and his rough, still-dirty hands. "It isn't my business, I know. But . . . You ain't just his groundskeeper, are you?"

She shook her head. He regarded her solemnly.

"Used to be a priest, didn't he?"

"Yes."

"But not anymore."

"No, that's over now."

He sat thinking for a while. "I never knew him all that well. He was younger. . . . My brother Graham's friend. He always struck me as snooty, spoiled, as a kid. Had that temper. But he had a rough life for a rich kid. I'll grant him that."

"What makes you say that?"

"I guess he must have told you about his father and all."

"No." She leaned forward and Burt looked stricken.

"*He* should tell you. I don't know that much about it."

"Just tell me what you know."

"We never saw much of Dr. Barlowe, when he was busy with that clinic of his, in Portland. Oh, sometimes Ma would call him in the middle of the night for emergencies and such. Boy, he was a mean, frosty old son of a bitch, even before he got sick. Excuse my language."

"Ellis did mention . . . he was difficult . . ."

"He'd actually yell at you for getting sick at the wrong time. Ma said he worked with the poor only because he couldn't get anyone else to go to him."

Rose shook her head.

"It's funny, because he was exactly like his father, the old parson: always angry, it seemed, lecturing you about something. But they never spoke to each other. There was a split, there."

"Dr. Barlowe didn't believe in God."

"That was probably it. And Reverend Barlowe didn't

even give his own son a burial. They had to do it up in Portland."

"How did he die, Burt?"

"I thought you knew. He had a cancer, terrible. In his gut. Must have been furious with himself for getting it. And instead of just staying in a hospital, like any normal person would, he made the son bring him back here. To die."

"Ellis took care of him."

"Yep. Couldn't have been easy. We heard there were no nurses, no housekeeper in that house. Only the boy. He must have been sixteen, seventeen then. You'd see him in town, doing the shopping, looking . . . Gosh, I felt sorry for him. Never liked him much, but he just looked so . . . tired, thin, like he was being run ragged. I'm sure the Doc wasn't giving him an easy time—" And then, Burt stopped talking. He actually placed his hand over his lips, as if to keep anything else from emerging, and Rose had the sense there was more.

"Go on, Burt," she prompted.

"He died." His voice was flat now. "And your Barlowe went off to college, and we never saw him again. Until now. It was a shock, the first time I saw him, in town. Grown up, a man, but he still has that look about him, I don't know, edgy, nervous. I can't figure it out, Rose. Why'd he come back here?"

Rose was shaken by the utter bafflement she heard in Burt's voice. "He says he has nowhere else to go." She drained her tea and set down her cup. "I should go now," she whispered. "See how he is." But she was filled with dread. Burt gave her a stern, almost angry look.

"Rose, you come here anytime you want. Anytime you need to, you just come."

She drove slowly, cautiously back toward the estate, just creeping along in the dark. She pulled up on the lawn, so he would not hear her tires crunching on the gravel driveway. But she was startled when he suddenly loomed before her, on the porch.

"Rose," he gasped. "Thank God." He reached for her, but she stepped backward abruptly, pulling herself out of his reach.

"Don't—" he pleaded, still reaching for her.

"You told me to leave!"

"I didn't mean it."

"Why'd you say it?"

"I don't know. I don't know what's wrong with me. I had one of my headaches . . . I couldn't think straight. Oh, Rose, I am so sorry. Please, please, don't go."

"I don't know if I can go on here, with you," she whispered, and his face crumpled, like a toddler's.

"Don't say that, Rose. If you leave me now, I . . . I couldn't go on. It's the truth. I couldn't—"

"No, no," she whispered, taking him in her arms. "It's not true, Ellis." He grasped her, gratefully, tearfully now. "You won't leave now, will you? Not yet?"

"Not yet," she said, with a sigh.

She let him draw her back into the house, and then to the bedroom. "No," she murmured, feebly, as he began to court her with delicate, pleading kisses, his own face still wet with tears. "No," she continued, even as she felt herself giving way, opening up to him.

And in making love with him, joining with him now, she felt as though she were making some profound, irreversible vow, linking with him, for life. She knew now she would never again try to leave him.

12

Rose was walking down the hospital corridor, toward the ICU, with Dr. Tan, her husband's distressingly young cardiologist: He seemed like a teenager to her, with a shock of boyish black hair, smooth skin, healthy smile, chinos and sneakers under his doctor's coat. He was probably in his thirties still, young enough to be her son. Time was, she thought, when all the men she knew and was connected with were older than she was, looming over her. She was beginning to feel like the oldest person in the world.

She liked Dr. Tan because of his optimism and cheerfulness; he explained the intricacies of her husband's heart and circulatory system with great enthusiasm and near-glee, and made even bad news seem good. But she always had to remind herself afterward just how serious Burt's condition really was—and that even the good news was almost always bad. Dr. Tan was chattering on now happily about the machine Burt was attached to.

"However, it appears now we won't be able to successfully wean him off the respirator," he concluded, with a quick, faintly apologetic little smile. Rose leaned toward him.

"Which means—"

"He's going to die. So that's what you and your family will have to decide. Whether to leave him on, indefinitely, or take him off. I'm sure you're familiar with this whole debate, about prolonging life, quality of life, et cetera. Man, it's all over the place, TV, newspapers. . . . Didn't he make out a living will, Mrs. Keating?"

"No, of course not. No one really believes they're going to die. Or in this manner."

Dr. Tan chuckled appreciatively. "That's so true! So true."

Rose stared at him balefully, wondering if she should be offended at his casual cheeriness. "Listen, Doctor. I . . . I know this sounds callous, but I have to go out of town for a few days . . ."

"Hey, no problem. I understand, life goes on. Mr. K isn't going anywhere."

"So I could go—"

"I'll give Mandy a buzz, if anything happens. Go, enjoy yourself. You can make the big decisions when you get back."

"Thank you," Rose murmured, turning away from him.

"Hey, Mrs. K?"

Rose turned.

"Is she dating anyone? Mandy, I mean."

Now she frowned at him, in a sharp, reprimanding way. Enough, she thought, was enough.

She was always surprised at how busy the intensive-care unit was: It was a buzzy, hivelike place that was always filled with voices, nurses and medical people scurrying about here and there, even laughter—not the dim, quiet womblike place depicted on television dramas. But somehow this gave her comfort: Burt always liked a commotion, and she felt easier leaving him in this busy, vital place for safekeeping until her return.

Burt lay on his back, his bed cranked up, eyes closed and sunk into his skull. The bottom part of his face was obscured by the breathing tubes and medical tape, so she ran her hand along his forehead, touching his closed eyelids. She wondered if she'd ever see those eyes open again, those bright blue eyes that reminded her of Caribbean seas.

"Hi Burt. It's Rose." She squeezed his hand, feeling faintly silly, absurd, as if she were literally conversing with a brick wall or a wooden trellis. She perched herself on his bed, setting her hip on the far corner, and it struck her that she would never again share a bed with him. She had not shared his bed in several years, not since the stroke; but she thought now of all the times she stayed up late to avoid going to bed with him. Of creeping carefully, delicately under the covers, struggling not to awaken him . . . or his desire for her.

He'd been good enough to wait for her, in the beginning, a whole year until after Mandy was born. It was a merciful gesture, for by the time they finally did join in bed, the memory of Ellis's skill and caresses had begun to fade, and the comparison between the two men was not so stark. Burt was not as clumsy or oafish a lover as she had feared he would be; but sex was a straightforward affair for him. It was quick, businesslike, silent. He lacked completely the sense of desperation or need that so aroused her with Ellis.

But that was never a role she expected Burt to fill: She saw him as simply a companion, a fellow farmer, a friend to provide consolation and steadiness and strength, things that Ellis could not offer. She knew there would be little passion or physical delight with Burt, yet she did not deny him her body—she felt she couldn't, as his legal wife. And it wasn't so bad, if she shut her eyes tightly and thought of Ellis. . . .

There had been unexpected rewards in their long life together: the sons who came in her forties, the rich family life they all shared, and the amazingly strong affection she developed for Burt over the years. They worked well together in the fields, in the store, at home, always presenting a united front to the children. Indeed, they rarely argued, a matter that pained her, when she thought about it: It only reminded her that as comfortable and companionable as her marriage to Burt was, there was no real passion or great depth of feeling in it; and she wondered if she'd cheated her husband out of something, after all.

"I hope I did make you happy, somehow . . ." she murmured now. "You never complained or showed any hurt. Any anger. A real soldier, that's what you were. A good father. A good husband—" She winced, thinking again of Ellis. Something that Ellis could never be to her: husband.

She leaned closer to him, whispering. "Burt. I have to go away for a few days. I'm really sorry, but it's important. Mandy will be here, and Tommy, and Hank, too. But I have to go. It's about . . . Ellis Barlowe." Her hand tightened on his shoulder. "You understand. You know how it is, how he is. He's run off again . . . I just have to find him and talk some sense into him, and I'll come right back, I promise." But even as she said this, a murky doubt began filling her. She had no idea what she would actually *do*, when she found Ellis. Stay with him, run away with him, somewhere else? Or bring him back— Could she actually do that, replace the outgoing Burt with Ellis? She closed her eyes. It was an impossible situation. But of course she could not say any of these things to Burt now; she could not send such thoughts into a dying man's brain. "You know how he is," she repeated. "Like a scared rabbit. I don't know what he's running from now."

The last time Ellis ran off, thirty years ago, he'd had the good grace to stop by her house first. She remembered her astonishment, finding him at her door, at 11 P.M., dressed not in clerical black but ordinary men's clothes, a sweater and slacks. *I'm going away,* he told her. *Can you pack up some of that tea for me, the tea you make for my headaches?*

Where are you going? she asked, mystified.

On vacation. It was not unusual or out of the ordinary: Parish priests had lives, too, family to visit, boats to sail and fish to catch. Golf or tennis to play. But something in his stiff stance, in the flatness of his voice alerted her.

Where?

I'm not sure yet, he murmured, evasively, looking away. But he watched intently as she scooped the dried leaves and bits of bark into a plastic bag.

What's in that tea, Rose? Can you write down the ingredients for me?

I could . . .

Do you have a tea for colds, too, for fevers, other illnesses? Of course.

Are there herbs that will put you to sleep?

Yes, yes, absolutely, there are teas to make you drowsy—

I meant, a permanent sleep.

A long eerie silence passed between them.

Why in the world would you ask that? she whispered. Again, he could not look at her. *I was just . . . curious.*

I don't know of any herbs like that, she lied, shaking inwardly.

I'm sure there are. His voice was soft, melancholy, his gray eyes empty. *You've just never had any reason to find them.*

She held the packet out to him, not knowing what to do or say next. He abruptly slid his hands around hers, squeezing them tightly.

Dear Rose. You are the only person in this entire town who has ever shown any real kindness to me.

She stared at him. She understood. He was going away and not coming back. If she let him go, she thought, he would go and find that fatal herb. Quick! She had to stop him somehow. She placed her hands on his chest, moving closer to him. He watched her, his lips parted, a look of vague alarm on his face. He was taller than she realized, so she had to crane her neck up, stand on her toes to reach his mouth with hers. And at first there was no response. Nothing. He felt stiff and cool to her, like cardboard. Inexperienced, she thought. But just as she was about to pull away, his mouth opened beneath hers, a soft moan escaping his lips.

In the morning, he was gone. She raced downstairs, clutching a sheet over her nakedness, and foolishly looked out the window, searching the street. But he was gone. Forever, she believed, despairingly. Until that phone call came from Maine.

Burt, forgive me, for thinking about such things with you lying here. She took his hand in hers: It felt distressingly dry, flaky, a dead thing, with yellowing, gnarled nails. She squeezed it, hoping to feel some life still in it, some response to her, some sign he'd heard her, however subtle or fleeting. She looked into his face and saw nothing there, no twitch or hint of life. When she leaned forward to kiss his cheek, she heard only the rhythmic hissing of his machine-induced breathing.

She left the hospital, with the uncomfortable feeling she was sneaking out, slinking away like a snake. She paused in the parking lot, thinking she should call Amanda one last time, check up on that boy Lucas. No, no, just go, leave right now, she thought: She had only a precious sliver of time in which to find Ellis. Each day, each moment that slipped away pushed him farther and farther from her.

She got into her truck and pulled out a road map. It was easier to get to Maine these days: There were swifter, better highways, more efficient ways to go, newer roads. If she were lucky, she could be there before dusk, perhaps in three or four hours.

13

ROSE awoke one morning to the sweet, overpowering scent of lilacs and the feeling of something grazing, tickling her chin and neck. She opened her eyes to find Ellis gazing down at her, gently stroking her face with a sprig of that very flower; by the bedside sat a huge quivering amethyst bouquet and she smiled, both delighted and touched by the unexpected gift.

"Summer's coming, for sure," he said, laying the sprig between her breasts, then kissing her in a long, deep, joyous sort of way. As if, she thought, the scent of the lilacs had infected him with some sort of euphoric summery fever.

"They're beautiful," she murmured. "A really old-fashioned variety. Where did you get them?"

"By the west edge of our property."

"Really? I never noticed lilacs there."

"They were the only flower that ever grew here, before." He nestled beside her. "My family never planted a thing, but they were just here. Grandmother said they were probably a hundred years old or so. She loved them, and I would pick a bunch for her, every spring. I picked some for her today, too."

She studied his face carefully. "You picked some . . . for her."

"Come with me. We'll take them over to her."

In the graveyard of the Wainscott Congregational Church, Ellis laid an armful of lilacs on his grandmother's grave with such elaborate tenderness Rose was moved almost to tears. He spread them out slightly in the space beneath the headstone, so that they formed a velvety protective sort of blanket over the grave.

"You loved her," Rose murmured. "I didn't think there was anyone in your family that you loved."

Ellis stood up. "If I had the power to raise anyone from the grave, she would be the only person I'd bring back. She was a gentle, decent woman. She couldn't really raise me: She was crippled with polio. But she did all these little things for me: Every winter I had a warm pair of mittens, and when I was at school she sent packages, cookies, treats, with notes and little poems tucked into them. During the summer, she'd watch me swim and applaud when I showed her all my different strokes. And when she felt up to it, I would assist her in the kitchen, and she would tell me tales of the old-time settlers, Pilgrim Barlowes. Little simple kindnesses. And even today, I'm amazed when anyone shows me any unexpected kindness; I can never believe I deserve it."

Rose took his arm, and they moved slowly from the graveyard to a small, adjoining park, where a group of small boys was playing ball. Ellis watched them for a while, and Rose struggled to understand the expression on his face: It seemed wistful, yearning. But for what?

"You must have been heartbroken when she died."

"I was, utterly bereft," he whispered. "I was only twelve; I didn't see how I'd go on without her."

A ball suddenly rolled toward them. Rose stepped forward and pitched it back, with a grin.

"You would make a good mother," he said, and she felt a sharp pang of sorrow and dismay.

"Did . . . do you *want* children, Ellis?" she ventured.

"I don't know what kind of father I would be. But I wish I could give you a child, Rose. I know it's not possible. But I wish I could give you something meaningful, in return . . ."

"Return? For what?"

"For your . . . care. For being here with me, remaining with me."

"Oh, Ellis. I don't need to have a child with you. It's enough just to be with you. Somehow, we'll create some kind of life for ourselves."

He gave her a wan, hopeful smile.

For days, the lilacs filled their bedroom with their magical scent, and Ellis's mood was warm, affectionate, almost buoyant. He seemed content with his reading, his work in the garden or on the house. He bought a small radio, so he could sit on the porch in the evenings and listen to the baseball games from Fenway Park. One day, returning from town, he brought an armload of newspapers and some magazines, as if he were suddenly interested in the world again. She actually spotted him poring over the "Help Wanted" ads, though with a distinctly disconcerted expression. Rose began to reimagine him as a "normal" man, growing comfortable, at ease within the temporal world, and her own spirits lifted as well.

But soon, the inevitable plague of the headache returned, and Ellis was plunged back into his own private Gethsemane: silent, rigid muscles, fingers digging into his temples as if he were actually trying to rip out the pain. Now once again he was rendered mute, motionless, cut off from the rest of the world.

She led him to the bedroom and drew the shades, then watched him for a while as he slept fully clothed, his tightly clenched face slowly relaxing into slumber. If she were married to him, would she always have to hover, watch over him so? Worry over him? Would he, in later years, evolve into a stronger, less troubled man, or would he always be haunted, hunted by matters still a mystery to her?

When she was certain that he was in a deep sleep, she reached into the pocket of his pants and drew out his key ring. There were his car keys, the key that opened the front door of the house, the barn's padlock key and a large, ornate Victorian iron key she suspected opened the massive front door of St. Cyril's church back in Wisterville.

She left the bedroom to fill a small box with tools, then headed upstairs. Once again, the ritual of removing the nails and the middle boards. She crawled through, into the world of dust and long-dead Barlowes, now made eerier by the setting sun, the rays of gold and rose tinting the walls and furnishings with a melancholy sort of glow. She knew that she was going against his wishes, but she needed to convince herself that nothing sinister lurked in the upstairs; and indeed, she detected nothing amid the shadows and niches that would concern or alarm, only old, delicate, decaying furniture, photographs of the deceased and long-gone. Once again, she jiggled the doors at the end of the hall, then tried to pry and wrench them apart with a variety of tools, all to no avail. She reached into the pocket of her trousers and brought forth her own keys: There was a skeleton key from her house in Wisterville. Idly, she inserted this into the lock, and the doors sprang open.

"Of all the crazy things," she muttered, pushing the doors aside; they glided smoothly into a wall pocket.

She swung the jittery, pale beam of an old flashlight

about the room, aiming a circle of light at the bookshelves, which overflowed with rare, old leatherbound books, the treasure that Edna, the antiques lady, had alluded to. She reached out and touched them with the tips of her fingers; the leather felt fragile, yet cool and stiff, like the skin of a dead person. She let the flashlight beam linger over the fireplace and the delft tiles set into the mortar: biblical scenes of Jacob and Esau, the prodigal son. The bed in the corner was an ordinary double bed, with the simplest of headboards. It was covered with an odd kind of spread, strangely modern, with an abstract design, dark shapes on white cotton. She moved closer, her hands touching the spread, the smoothness of the fabric, except where the pattern began, a dull, brownish splatter, stiff to the touch—

Her hand darted away. For a moment, she could barely breathe, her head spinning. She snapped the flashlight off and backed out of the room, slamming the sliding doors closed again, firmly.

She let Ellis sleep all night and late the next morning. She wanted to work out in the garden by herself, in the coolness before midday. She needed to think, to sort things out. To understand. Sometimes the dull, repetitive work of weeding helped, sometimes not. She found her mind a blur of images. She kept seeing those muddy-brown spots and splatters, a long crescent streak down the length of the bed. . . . How could someone just leave a room like that, a horror waiting to be discovered? It was beyond her comprehension.

"Rose?"

She looked up to find him standing over her. His face was pinched in concern.

"Your headache—?"

"It's gone." He knelt, coming down to her level, his face near hers. "What's wrong?" His tone was oddly solicitous, even paternal.

"Nothing's wrong."

"You seem so preoccupied. You didn't wake me this morning."

"No, I wanted to be alone. Can't I be alone, if I want?"

He studied her in a worried way. "I'm sorry. I know I'm not the easiest man to live with. I know I've hurt you—"

"I'm fine, Ellis. I just wish . . . you were more honest with me. About yourself, your life. Your past." The image of the bed was still swirling about in her head, before her eyes, and yet somehow she couldn't bear to mention it, to speak of it directly. She almost didn't want to know, or hear, his explanation.

"What . . . what did you need to know?" His tone was brave, but he looked distraught now, even frightened. She felt a wave of pity.

"Your father . . . died, upstairs? Is that why—"

"Yes, yes," he whispered. "I can't go up there. Not yet. You understand, don't you, Rose? How painful certain memories can be?"

"Yes, of course, Ellis. I won't badger you about it. But I can't help but think . . . it seems wrong for you to be here."

"This is my home." His tone was both regretful and full of a stubborn sort of pride. "I won't be chased from it by phantoms or memories. Please don't think I'm deliberately hiding anything from you, Rose. But there are things I can't talk about yet. Things I haven't sorted out. Things I don't understand myself."

She nodded, without looking up at him, feeling at an impasse.

"Rose, I do have something to tell you. Something that's not easy to say."

She stretched her arms out, bracing herself. Bracing herself against the earth for yet another blow. "Just say it," she murmured, and she felt his breath against her cheek, her ear.

"I love you." A fearful sort of admission; the shyness and terror in it moved her. Still, unbelieving, she looked at him suspiciously.

"I do. I love you, Rose. I've never actually said that to anyone. I've never had any reason to say it to anyone. Before now." He paused, tilting his head slightly. "Don't you believe me?"

"I never thought I'd ever hear it," she murmured. "From you."

"I do love you, Rose. Rose?" He gathered her grimy hands in his, and looked at her expectantly, anxiously, his gray eyes searching her face in a hungry way. Waiting, she thought, for her to say it, too. But she *couldn't*. Her brain would not send the words down into her mouth. Her mouth would not open. Oh, she felt it: She burned and ached with love for him, was weary with the effort of loving him. But somehow, she could not tell him. She saw a crestfallen look on his face, his storm-cloud eyes searching hers, desperately, and she swiftly slid her arms around him, hoping to communicate with tight embrace, with kisses, the things her brain would not let her say.

14

Lucas and Rose's son Tommy sat slumped on a sofa in front of TV, two adult men drinking milk and eating from a bag of cookies, amid a background of bright, noisy chatter and tinny laughter. Lucas, brushing a trail of crumbs off his sweater, felt exactly like his ten- or twelve-year-old self again, but it was neither a pleasant nor comforting feeling: He had the sense of having skipped over adulthood, jumping straight from adolescence into the odd kind of childhood provided by the monastery, a chaste and severely disciplined boyhood in which he was ordered around by older, fatherly monks. His own childhood had been far less orderly, his parents always out and about, consumed with their own lives; his only real monitor had been the indifferent Hispanic housekeeper who dragged him and his siblings to church every Sunday.

He cringed when a commercial came on, set in a shadowy abbey full of dark, silent monks. One of them began to mug and dance about cartoonishly, singing about some product—telephone service? Corn chips? Lucas turned his eyes away, as if he were taking part in some sort of betrayal just by watching.

"That's all we're reduced to in the modern world," he muttered. "Anachronistic buffoons, hawking senseless garbage."

"Huh?" said Tommy.

"No one in this world understands the monastic life," Lucas continued, more to himself than his companion.

Tommy looked blank for a moment, then nodded his head sagely. A coping mechanism, thought Lucas. Or maybe he did understand, after all. Lucas imagined Tommy's retardation had imposed a sort of involuntary monasticism on him: He might be forever silent, and chaste. He would fit in beautifully at the abbey, thought Lucas, working tirelessly in the fields, singing chants and collecting herbs from Theo's gardens. Tending to the ill, without wrinkling his nose or cringing. No complex, disturbing, warring thoughts to wreck his calm.

The kitchen's screen door slammed: Amanda, returning from her vigil by Burt's hospital bed. Lucas caught a brief, unguarded glance at her in the hallway: He saw a somewhat weary, worried, vaguely mournful thirty-year-old woman wearing a simple printed dress, running a distracted hand through her hair. But as she entered the TV room, her face drew back into its cool, scornful-temptress look, with narrow cat's eyes and twisted smile.

"Well, boys. Not such a swell way to spend a Saturday night."

Tommy giggled. Obviously he enjoyed, even adored, his older sister on some level, thought Lucas with surprise. He watched as Amanda playfully grabbed a hank of Tommy's hair and tugged at it, Tommy protesting happily. Lucas himself came from a large family, but all his sisters and brothers seemed similar in temperament and intelligence. There seemed such a huge variance among individual members of the Keating family, he could not imagine how they formed a loving, cohesive unit. Amanda plopped onto Tommy's lap and grabbed her brother's cheeks— Until that moment, Lucas had not realized how petite she was, or perhaps, how large Tommy was.

"Go to bed, stupid," she told him, tenderly. "You have a lot of work to do tomorrow, after church."

After Tommy stumbled off amiably, Amanda turned her attention to Lucas. "What about you?"

"I've been sleeping all day! And look what happened. Your mother snuck off for Maine without me!"

"You wanted to go with her?"

"That was the whole reason I left the abbey! To help her find him!"

She studied him with a piercing sort of look, her head half-cocked, as if trying to see through him: another eerie identical-Theo look. He still had not gotten used to her resemblance to Theo, and this did not ease the discomfort he felt in her presence. He was rarely comfortable in the presence of women—Rose was a notable exception—particularly young women, who distressed him for reasons he could not name. It occurred to him that Amanda had Theo's intelligence, perhaps, and maybe even his intuition, certainly his sharp tongue, prickly temper and coolness; but he was sure she lacked his heart and compassion.

"I need to find him, too," he added, with emphasis.

"Why?" Amanda seemed amused now. "Does he owe you money?"

"Theo was my teacher, my mentor. But he was also an extraordinary human being. He has patients, dying men who are dependent on him for comfort, for aid, for his remedies. He has to go back to the monastery."

"That's interesting. I don't think those are the plans my mother has for him at all."

"That's why I should have gone with her."

She peered at him. "What about your family? Shouldn't you be giving them a call?"

He shrugged in bafflement and dismay.

"Are they so awful, Lucas? Your folks?"

For a long moment he didn't answer; he hoped the silence would answer for him, but Amanda's questioning stare did not waver. He took out his wallet—an absurd thing, he thought, for a monk to carry, for he had no cash, no credit cards—and pulled out a photograph: an old photo snapped for one of his father's campaign brochures.

"A big family," she murmured. "And your father's a . . . big man. Huge. You don't resemble him at all."

"Yes, that was the family joke. I didn't look like anyone else. Dad actually joked I was really the milkman's or mailman's kid."

"Were you?"

"Of course not. But I never felt like his son. There's really no connection there, between us."

"There's no mother in this picture."

"No, my mother was dead by then. I was closer to her."

Amanda tilted the photo, her head tilted at the same angle, her eyes moving back and forth from the photo to Lucas, as if she were trying to come to some sort of conclusion about him.

"Your mother is dead, and you don't get along with your father."

"No one 'gets along' with Myles Reardon. You either do his bidding, or completely ignore him. He's a bully," Lucas said casually, with no bitterness in his voice. "He's an honest, decent, churchgoing man, but a bully nonetheless. He won't be pleased at all to see me back on his doorstep, but that's not what I'm afraid of. It's what he may try to make me do next. Probably something involving law." Lucas grimaced. Of course, he left out the gay issue, that whole messy, unspoken matter between him and Myles. But he did not want to discuss his sexuality with the sharp-tongued, and perhaps unsympathetic, Amanda.

"So, what are you going to do now?" she asked.

"I don't know. I . . . I don't know that there's a place for me in this world. I might have no choice but to return to Benedetto. At least there I have a job: duties, things that I'm good at."

"But you don't really want to go back?"

Not without Theo, he thought. But instead, he countered: "What do *you* want to do?"

"What?" She was thrown, and he felt a twinge of satisfaction.

"You're not going to spend the rest of your life living here on this farm with your mother, are you?"

"Why not?" she said in an airy way. "It's not such a bad life." But he was sure he detected impatience and irritation in her voice.

"You really don't seem the type. You know, a spinster."

Now she laughed. "I'm not. Thanks for noticing." She beckoned for him to follow her out into the hallway. "Come into the living room. There's something I want to show you."

He studied the photographs displayed on the living room wall: the Keating children as babies, as toddlers, as schoolchildren. Rose and Burt in ordinary clothes, but striking a formal pose: their wedding day? Burt was grinning, happy, but Rose, carrying a bouquet, seemed serious, her expression distant. Other shots of her were happier: vacation pictures, picnics, the family gathered about the Christmas tree. One big happy family. Lucas frowned. It was clear to him Rose had gotten her fair share in life. A huge farm, successful business, loving, if prickly, children. A husband who probably adored her. Why then, did she need Theo? He felt a dart of anger, annoyance. It occurred to him that Rose was being greedy in some way.

He stared at a grouping of Amanda photos: in pigtails, as a white-robed graduate, long blond hair streaming down her back, and then—

"Is this you? In an . . . army uniform?"

"Yes. I went in right after high school."

"Wow. Why'd you join the army?"

"Why did you enter the monastery?"

They glanced at each other, then smiled, coming to a silent understanding about loving but difficult families and the need to escape.

"Did you like it?" he asked.

"It was okay. I was trained as a mechanic. I had a weird knack for it. But when I came out and tried to get a job, it was a joke. Trying to get a job at a garage with my looks? No guy would hire me, nobody believed I could do it. But I didn't want one of those girl-jobs, sitting in an office all day. I worked for the phone company for a while, shimmying up poles. But I got bored with that. I even drove a trailer truck for a while, cross-country, but that wasn't right, either. I don't have much of an attention span, I guess. Restless, my mother says."

"And now you haven't a clue what to do next."

"Did I say that?" she snapped. "I'm here for a reason, you know. In case you forgot, my father is dying."

He stared at her: Did she even know that Theo—Ellis—Barlowe was her biological father?

"And when he dies?"

She blinked in indignation. "I'm not thinking beyond that point yet. Anyway"—she pulled a thick black binder from a nearby bookcase—"this is what I wanted to show you. I think you might find it of interest." There was a

playful, teasing quality in her voice he didn't understand.
He frowned, taking the binder from her and opening it.

Maine, 1965.

Puzzled, he began flipping slowly through the book. It
seemed to be a collection of botanical drawings, various
flowers and herbs, each sketch carefully dated. He glanced
at Amanda, who was grinning in an infuriating way. A few
pages later, he came upon a hand. Just a hand, with no
identifying label, but Lucas recognized it instantly: long,
slender fingers, bony, protuberant knuckles, clean, neatly
clipped nails.

"Yes," he whispered.

A few pages later he came upon Theo complete, a
younger, achingly handsome Theo in summery clothes,
short-sleeved shirt and swim trunks. How odd to see him
in such ordinary attire, perched on a porch railing . . . with
a cigarette in his hand? Lucas raised his eyebrows. He was
reading, engrossed in a big thick book that sat on his lap,
and despite the casual clothes, the cigarette in his hand,
there was an oddly stark, touchingly bookish, monastic
quality about the picture that made Lucas yearn to rip it
out and keep it for himself.

"Keep turning." Amanda stood over him, her blond
pageboy swinging, her gray eyes filled with a malicious sort
of merriment.

"The best is yet to come."

He glanced up at her warily. "Go ahead," she prompted,
sinking beside him in the armchair, their hips touching,
shoulder to shoulder. He felt her hair brush up against his
face, as he turned the page.

"Oh," he moaned, in surprise and dismay. There was
Theo, asleep in bed, utterly naked. Lucas averted his eyes,
while Amanda's laughter trilled beside him.

"Is that him? Your Theo, or whatever you call him?"

Lucas forced himself to look at the picture. It was very

innocuous, really, nothing pornographic or sinister about it at all. Theo caught deep in slumber, his head thrown back, revealing a long, swanlike neck, his mouth partly open and limbs thrown out—Rose was careful to define the muscles of his shoulders, his stomach, his legs. Also drawn with great delicacy were his genitals, the un-erect but impressive penis casually lying across his thigh. Lucas allowed himself a brief erotic shudder, then slammed the book shut.

"Lucas?" Amanda asked, with some concern.

"I don't know him. I don't know him at all."

"It's not your Theo?"

"It is. I just don't know who he is, at all."

"Neither do I. And he *fathered* me."

"I thought so," he murmured, staring at the floor. "You really do resemble him enormously. I almost fell over when I saw you."

"Really?" She slid down onto the floor, so she was at his feet, staring up at him, her face filled with a girlish sort of curiosity. "Do I really look so much like him? Rose never said."

"You've never met him? You never saw a photograph?"

"Mom has no photographs. Only these." She patted the book on his lap. "When I was growing up, I knew that I looked like no one in the family. At first I thought I was adopted, but then I heard Mom describe the horrible labor she went through with me. So then I decided I must be a throwback to her Ukrainian ancestors."

"When did you learn the truth?"

For a moment she didn't answer, looking away from him.

"Oh, I had suspicions. I'd be a dope not to, wouldn't I?" She laughed in a casual but vaguely wounded way that Lucas found touching. "Not from Burt, dear old Burt, he loved me as much as he loved his boys. Maybe even more. Mom never said a word. All her secrets, she kept so much from us. I did see these pictures once. Mom used to keep them upstairs in her room, away from us. I came upon them and looked at them, looked at *him*, but I didn't make the connection then. And Mom was writing to this mysterious man all the time, way out in Pennsylvania, but he was just an old priest, it never occurred to me . . . well, she did tell me, finally. Finally she told me the truth . . . on the morning of my wedding. Yeah, I was married, briefly. I guess she thought telling me this secret on the Big Day would somehow bring us closer. But it didn't. I was furious. And sick— I actually threw up. I couldn't believe Burt Keating wasn't my father. I cried as I walked up the aisle with him clutching my arm. I guess it set the tone for my marriage."

Lucas felt a twinge of pity for her and a gradual reversal of his feelings for her: In her confessional mode, she seemed softer, gentler; her eyes were cast down demurely.

"I guess you and your mom," he ventured, "don't really get along too well."

"It's not her fault. I'm not an easy person to get along with." A dry laugh. "Ask my ex-husband."

"Does she love Burt? Or did she marry him just to forget Ellis?" Theo's worldly name felt strange in his mouth, but he had wanted to try it out. Amanda shrugged.

"I don't know. I honestly don't know. I always thought she did. She gave the appearance of loving him, being a good wife. But now with this weird obsession of hers suddenly coming out now, I just don't know what to think."

"How did they meet? Do you know?"

"No, no. Mom never went into it. All I know is that she loved this crazy man once, and never quite got over it. I also know"—she grinned up at him—"he doesn't know the truth about me."

"Don't you want to meet him? Aren't you curious about him?"

"No," she barked, her face like stone.

"Not even a little?"

"Burt is my father. And Burt is dying. I can't talk about another man right now. A man who didn't even have the decency to support my mother, or marry her and raise his own child."

"But he didn't know!" Lucas argued.

"Don't defend him!" Amanda snapped. "Why are *you* so interested in him?"

"I told you, he was—"

"Yeah, yeah, extraordinary." Her eyes searched his face. "You wouldn't happen to have some kind of crazy crush on him yourself, would you?"

"No," he lied, feeling like St. Peter before the cock's crow. "No. But he is . . . irreplaceable. There is no other monk who can accomplish what he does, who works as hard as he does, no one who listens and consoles the way he does—"

"My God, he's a saint." To Lucas's ears, Amanda's tone was pure sarcasm, cynical belittlement. He turned to confront her, his mouth opening in outrage. But instead found himself staring at her—her gray-blue eyes, and the angular, so-familiar shape of her face, even the shape of her mouth, the shape of her grin—and a crazy, helpless laughter began bubbling up inside him, bubbling out, the sort of inappropriate laughter that emerges at funerals and solemn Masses. Her grin was replaced with something more benign, a kind of delighted surprise; her eyes lit up.

"What? What is it, Lucas? What's so funny?"

He laughed again, imagining the shock of the smug abbot and the older monks upon seeing this provocative young woman with her amazing resemblance to Theo. "You should come up to Benedetto and visit sometime."

She squeezed his knees triumphantly. "You're actually laughing! This is the first time I've seen you smile. You have an adorable smile, you're really a cute guy, Lucas. Luke." She leaned her chin on his kneecap. "Why did you go in?"

she asked, in a gentler way. "What were you running away from?"

"Nothing." He felt confused now, alarmed and strangely thrilled by her laughter, her proximity to him. "Nothing. You tell me, first. What you're running away from."

She drew back. Cold again, suddenly. "I'm not the one running away."

"I think you are."

"Is this monk-talk? Are you trying to get me to bare my soul?"

"No, but if you're going to pry into my business—"

"Look, my parents need me here, now. Can't you see that? I can't go off and do anything now."

"But this is a temporary situation for you."

"Of course it is. But I have to stay here, now." She paused. "For Burt. He needs me, because Mom has abandoned him. I'm not talking about this trip to Maine. Ever since he had his first stroke, she's been withdrawing, pulling away from him. It's as if she'd been waiting her whole life for this to happen. I'd swear she can't wait for him to die. Maybe it's all because of this Ellis guy, who knows. But my father, my real father, Burt, deserves better. I'm sure he can still feel things, Lucas, sense things. I have to be there for him."

"And when he's gone?"

"And if Rose doesn't find your Theo?" she countered.

"Guess we're in the same boat. Stalled, waiting for direction."

"I do have some idea," she said, in a small, childlike voice. "I will go somewhere, start all over again. But there have been so many so-called fresh starts in my life, new beginnings that don't work out. I feel like a car that keeps surging ahead, then stopping cold. How do I know the next fresh start will work out?"

"What's the alternative? Stay here forever?"

"Have you thought about going into counseling?" She was mocking him again. "You have the face for it. Sweet, open, trusting."

"Maybe I'll just go back to Benedetto," he said, morosely.

"Do you want to?"

"I don't know, Amanda. I don't know."

"Maybe you should just stay out in the world a bit. You know, check it out. Try some things. You can always go back, can't you? I mean, after a few years? They won't black-ball you or anything, will they?"

"I don't think so, but—"

"You ever have a girlfriend?" She laid a hand on his thigh, and he was mortified—astonished!—to feel himself stiffen, grow aroused. It must be her face, he thought: her Theo-ness. He shook his head no to her question, and she grinned, obviously pleased.

"Don't you ever wonder, what *that's* like? What you're missing?" She leaned closer to him. "Don't you feel like you want to burst?" she whispered fiercely, and in response he simply turned away from her, his face burning.

"I'm sorry, I've embarrassed you." But she didn't sound sorry in the least, only vastly amused. "But you must think about it, how can you not? How can you ignore an entire part of your body?"

"When," he managed to ask, "do you think your mother will be back?"

She seemed saddened by the change in topic. "I don't know, Lucas." Mercifully, she stood up, sobered. "So what are you going to do for the time being? Stay on here?"

He threw up his hands helplessly. "I think I have to. Until I get some word about Theo."

15

H<small>E'D</small> said it: Ellis said he loved her. Now she sat at the kitchen table that evening in mid-July, pondering her future with him. But she felt no real joy or anticipation, only puzzlement, a sense of worry. Ellis had gone down to Portland with a boxful of antiques to sell, and she was grateful for the time alone to think. About the bloodied bed in the attic—just above her head, now—about his moodiness and seeming inability to share anything substantial about his past with her. Was it, as he'd claimed once, so unimportant, not worth discussing? Did it really have anything to do with their lives now, their love for each other? Wasn't he, indeed, healing, growing stronger before her eyes, his headaches and foul moods less frequent? And he'd taken the amazing step of declaring his love. She knew that had not been easy for him: She herself could not even mouth the words yet, say them aloud. Why not? What was holding her back? She had no idea: Only some vague worry, some sense of unease. A faint suspicion, maybe, that Ellis might eventually hurt or betray her. She was nearly forty, too old or too wise to believe completely in fairy-tale romances, happily ever after. She looked up from the table and was startled to see Burt Keating's large, lumbering frame just outside the screen door. He shrugged apologetically when he saw her. In his arms, he had several pots, each containing a small, fanlike plant.

"Oh, irises," she murmured with pleasure, feeling grateful for the distraction.

"Yep. Purple and blue, mostly. We're working on a pink one. Graham is, that is. He's the genius of the family." She saw him looking around, his eyes scanning the kitchen in a wary way.

"Ellis is gone," she assured him. "Off to Portland, or somewhere. I was just about to have dinner." She peered at him. "Have you eaten yet, Mr. Keating?"

He actually blushed pink under the smudges of dirt on his face. "Why, no. Are you . . . are you asking me for dinner, Mrs. Connolly?"

"I have this chicken stew in the freezer. Ellis doesn't care for it. And a salad. And bread, baked just this morning. I'd be grateful if you joined me."

Burt could not seem to believe his luck. He ate happily, noisily, and heartily. He hadn't taken the time to wash his hands, but it didn't bother her: She knew it was only farm dirt, honest dirt, and she was not unduly bothered by his scent of mud and fertilizer and perspiration. He'd removed his cap; his forehead was a pale smooth band between the coppery hair and reddened face. She found herself looking at his hands, so different from Ellis's, comically oversize, stubby calloused fingers, mauling a slice of bread. It was hard to imagine such hands on a woman's body: Those fingers would poke, stab rudely, she thought, into the most delicate areas.

"Have you ever been married, Burt?"

He gave her a sheepish look. "Once. Years ago. Didn't work out." He chomped noisily, his bright blue eyes thoughtful. "Girl from Damariscotta. Too young. She ran away, after just three weeks. Some other guy."

"Oh. How tragic."

He shrugged. "I guess I'm not really one for the ladies." He grinned ruefully at his big chapped hands, the dirt ground in so deep Rose doubted they'd ever completely come clean. He looked up at her.

"So what happened to Mr. Connolly? You leave him for this Barlowe?"

"No. I'm a widow. My husband died some time ago."

"What of?"

She paused. "Well, he was very ill. Mentally. I tried to help him, had him in and out of hospitals. He finally took his own life. His doctors said there was nothing I could have done to prevent it."

He nodded. "That's probably the truth. Once a fellow makes up his mind to die, that's usually it. Just like old Doctor Barlowe, I guess. Nothing you can do or say—"

"Doctor Barlowe committed suicide?"

Burt seemed chastened by her alarm. "Thought you knew that."

"No, Ellis never told me. How awful."

"He probably didn't want you to know," Burt grumbled.

"I can't see why not. Though to be honest, I never told him about my husband. . . . Oh, poor Ellis. How did . . . How did Doctor Barlowe *do* it, do you know?"

Burt seemed irritated now. "I don't really know anything about it, Rose. Only what we read about in the papers."

"And what did they say?"

"Some kind of overdose, I think."

"An . . . overdose," Rose murmured. "Medicine."

"Yeah. But I don't really know. It was so long ago. We were just kids, all of us, then."

Rose let him eat for a while, her own portion of stew untouched.

"What was Ellis like as a boy?"

"I didn't know him so well, Rose." Burt frowned into his stew.

"You grew up just down the road, down the beach. You're about the same age."

"He wasn't here much. They sent him to that boarding school down in New Hampshire, and his dad kept him busy. Sometimes we'd see him in the summertime. He'd come down to the ball field. He tried hard to be normal, one of the boys. But he wasn't. He was shy, you could see that. Forcing himself to talk to us. But at the same time his nose in the air, so superior. And that temper of his. You could ask my brother Graham about that. How Ellis broke his arm, nearly killed him."

"Why would Ellis do that?" Rose whispered. To her astonishment, Burt blushed bright red and averted his eyes.

"They got into a fight."

"What about?"

"Barlowe said . . . my brother made a pass at him. . . ." Rose blinked, in confusion.

"I guess we all assumed he was . . . I guess my brother did, too. My brother is, you know. Queer, homosexual, whatever you call it."

"Ellis certainly is not."

"Ain't you proof of that. Well, your Ellis went right at him, hit him first, defending his manhood, I guess. Graham managed to get in a good swing, caught him right here—" He fingered the bridge of his own nose. "Graham never talked much about it afterward, but he did say once he thought Barlowe had 'led him on.'"

"I find that hard to believe."

"I think what Barlowe really wanted from him," Burt

said, suddenly, in a melancholy way, "was just to be friends. That boy really needed a friend, and there wasn't anybody on the island who could be. Because he didn't fit in. Even if he lived here, he wasn't one of us, he was always . . . apart. On his own."

"You felt sorry for him?"

"Oh, sure, Rose. I still do. A man like that . . . never really finds his way in the world, you know?"

She actually found herself nodding, wincing inwardly as she did so.

"Though I guess I'm not one to talk, a worthless old bachelor like me."

She leaned forward. "What about his mother? Do you know anything about her?"

"Not much. She didn't last too long here. She was a Canuck, you know, one of those French girls. One of Dr. Barlowe's charity cases, a teenager."

"A teenager?"

"Maybe sixteen, seventeen, my mother said. And pregnant already, before she got here. One of Dr. Barlowe's mistakes, they said. There were always rumors about him and the girls he treated at his clinic in the city. Ma said this one was a real beauty, though. A pretty blond, little, petite. Ma also said the boy—that's Ellis—favored her in looks. But she also put on airs, too, they said, and refused to learn English. She only spoke French and went to the Catholic Church every Sunday. Which was sort of a slap in the face to her father-in-law."

"I would imagine so." Rose was intrigued. "What happened to her?"

"Figure it out yourself. Doc Barlowe was a sour old bachelor, already in his forties, maybe fifties. She was just a kid. You can't imagine something like that would work out."

"I was under the impression she'd died."

Burt seemed astonished. "Did Barlowe tell you that?" Before she could answer, he jumped in: "I find it hard to believe he hasn't told you any of this."

"Ellis won't talk about his family."

"Can't say I blame him. Them being so odd. Still, he should . . . tell you some things. This is a small island, a small town. Did he think you were never going to meet anyone here, talk to anyone? Didn't he think you'd hear the rumors?"

"What rumors?"

He seemed nervous. "Oh, you know. Gossip."

"Such as—?"

"Oh, folks always talked about the Barlowes. The old doctor, doing himself in like that. Then Ellis running off, first to the service, then into the priesthood. Now, leaving that, coming here. With you. I hate to say it, but you two are the talk of the town."

"I suppose we are," she said, regretfully. "I suppose we're the talk of Wisterville, Connecticut, too. But up here, I always had the sense of being protected . . . cloistered off, cut off from the rest of the world. I guess that's not possible in any community of people."

They shared a moment of silence. Burt finished his stew. "I imagine Barlowe will have some tales to tell you. When he's good and ready to tell them."

She sent him home with the rest of the stew and the remainder of the day's bread, then carefully cleaned the kitchen, so no trace of his presence remained, though when she took a deep breath, she could still smell the scent of earth and sweat, another, different sort of male aroma. She opened all the windows wide and put on a small fan in the kitchen.

Ellis arrived home less than an hour later. He walked into the kitchen and paused, throwing a brief, inquiring look at Rose, and something in his face—a tightening, a paleness—alerted her.

"Headache?" she asked, quietly.

"Just a touch . . . Rose, was someone here?"

"No." She felt a flush spread across her face: She hated lying to him. He studied her face for a long moment, then moved slowly past her, onto the porch. He did not pick up his book, but leaned against the railing, staring out to sea.

"Would you like some tea?"

"No, I took some aspirin . . ." She saw him turn his head slightly and stare down at the potted irises, now lined neatly along the edge of the porch. His gaze returned to her.

"You're holding back something from me," he whispered, a look of betrayal spreading across his face. She felt a warm flush, an odd mix of remorsefulness and anger. "I forgot," she snapped. "You're the only one allowed to have secrets, keep things back."

"What are you keeping from me?"

"Oh, good heavens. Burt Keating brought me some irises. He just showed up, Ellis, and I didn't want to mention his name to you."

"That's it? That's all . . . only irises?"

She met his gaze defiantly, but kept her mouth closed, not wanting to lie again.

"I don't want him here again," said Ellis in a low, hurt voice.

"Now *you* tell me something. Don't tense up, Ellis. I only want to ask . . . about your mother." Her voice dropped to a soft, pleading tone. "I lost my mother, too, when I was little. I don't even have a memory of her, not even a photo. Is that it, Ellis? You have no memories of your mother? Is that why you never talk about her?"

He shut his eyes. "She used to . . . wear her hair like yours. Braided, sometimes, or coiled up, in the back. It was blond. She was . . . beautiful."

"You do remember her."

"I do remember. Going to church with her, every Sunday." He folded his arms, then suddenly hugged himself, his back now to the sea. "To her church. So different from Grandfather's church. Ornate, dark, mysterious. She used to wear this black veil over her blond hair. Odd, isn't it, the things we remember, the things stuck in our brains." He smiled faintly. "I remember her bringing me to what must have been midnight Mass, at Christmas. I remember waking up on her lap, in her arms, inhaling the smell of her wool coat and perfume, and the incense . . . hearing the choir and organ. . . ." His eyes moved upward. "I remember the windows, the stained-glass windows were black, colorless, and how strange it was, to be in church in the middle of the night. Strange, but wonderful."

"How touching," she murmured.

"Yes, very touching." He gave her a swift, cynical grin, and she was mystified.

"She had these terrible headaches. Like the ones I get now. She'd lie on her bed, and she'd look so pale, as if she were going to die. And she wept a lot. I was so terrified for her, so worried . . . even as a little boy, I had an awful, ominous sense of what was going to happen. That she was going to leave me. And then sometime after my fifth birthday, she disappeared. My father sat me down and told me she had died." Ellis shuddered. "I knew what that meant, I'd already seen dead people, and later my father showed me more on his rounds at his clinic. I knew that she could never come back. We no longer spoke of her, no one did: not my father, nor my grandparents, nor the neighbors. And if I mentioned her or spoke of her everyone froze up, and the subject would be changed. I even asked once if I could visit her grave. 'You cannot,' my grandfather said. 'She's far away, back with her own people.' " His words were coming quicker, faster, as if forced out from his throat; he was breathless. "I was never allowed to go back to her church, of course, but I did, secretly. I read Catholic books in private and made secret plans to join the priesthood, as soon as I could. I was sure my mother would have wanted that. I was so certain she was up there, in heaven, looking down at me. Beaming with love, with approval." He paused, then suddenly laughed aloud, an angry, bitter laugh.

"In heaven. And all the time, she was in *Bangor*, living with another man. Another family. She was *alive*, Rose, she never died, she merely walked out. On my father, on me. And left town, never to contact us again. My whole priestly career, the impetus for my vocation, was all based on a silly myth, a fairy tale of a saintly woman who died too young."

"How did you find out?"

"I might never have known. I was too wrapped up in my own vision, or version, of her, but apparently it was known in town. People knew of her, knew what had become of her. But no one saw fit to share that with me until . . . she actually did die. I was a priest already, an assistant curate down in Providence. Someone—maybe a neighbor, a distant relation—sent me a newspaper clipping of her obituary. I was actually listed as one of her survivors: 'A son, Ellis Jonathan Barlowe, of Wainscott, Maine.'" He stared down at his palm, as if the item were imprinted there. "To say I was stunned would be an understatement. I was sitting in my office at the rectory, a young couple in front of me, waiting to be counseled. I literally could not speak. I got up and just walked out of the room. Even now," his voice dropped, "I can't understand why she abandoned me like that."

"Perhaps . . . your father forbade her to see you?"

"No. No. He wouldn't have done that. He could be very difficult, cold and unloving at times. But he was fair. He never mentioned her, which makes me think she hurt him badly in some way. As for me, I think she did love me. But not enough."

"She was so young, Ellis, too young to be a mother, a wife—" It was too late to snatch her words back. Ellis stared at her in disbelief.

"How did you know *that?*"

"I . . . guess I heard it. In town."

"Yes," he said, drily. "People do talk about us."

"Oh, Ellis. She should have sought you out. Any decent mother would have."

He rubbed his left temple, the birthplace, it seemed, of all his migraines.

"When I found out about her, I felt as if the earth had been kicked out from under me. I'd been through a lot already in my life, but it was the last straw. I never quite felt the same about my vocation again. And yet, I don't know that leaving it was the answer, either."

She felt a chill, but said nothing.

"That's why it was so hard, so frightening, to tell you that I'd fallen in love with you. Because it was—it is—a real step away from that life. I could not go back so easily now."

She took his hands. "Ellis, we shouldn't stay here. We should go somewhere else."

He stared at her, his gray eyes wide with pain and bafflement. "There's nowhere else to go, Rose. Nowhere on this earth."

16

THE wooden washboard bridge to Wainscott Island was long gone, replaced by a sleek concrete span that curved out from the mainland. Rose paused at the eastern edge of the bridge, looking out over the bay, then—swiftly, fearfully—at the steep downhill road behind her. She continued on, her heart thumping wildly.

She saw that the marshes were partially filled in by either developers or nature and were dotted with "cottages" of what seemed to be ridiculous proportions to her, newly sided, with skylights, gables and faux Palladian windows.

She was forced to slow down as she entered the town of Wainscott itself, finding herself in a mini traffic jam. She swallowed hard, looking around, trying to find some old familiar landmark for her eyes to latch onto: There was the marina, busy now, crowded with boats and yachts of every description; and she was relieved to see the spire of old Parson Barlowe's Congregational Church, and the gingerbread Catholic Church a block away. But the rest of the town had undergone a stunning—and to Rose, deeply disconcerting—transformation, sprawling, multiplied into dozens and dozens of small, fussy storefronts, each selling, it seemed, the exact same sort of merchandise: T-shirts, kites, folk art, baskets, dried flowers. A few fancy little cafés and bistros had been sandwiched in, and the sidewalks—there were actually sidewalks now—were crowded with summer browsers. Traffic slowed to a halt, and Rose scanned the crowds on the street, her grip tightening when she thought she saw a tallish man, white-haired, who might be Ellis's age, walking along, hands in pockets. The car in front of her moved a few inches and when she looked back, he was gone, swallowed up by the crowd.

How would she ever find Ellis? In her mind, Wainscott had remained unchanged, a remote, quiet, decidedly unfashionable seaside town. She and Burt had never returned, not even for a visit. Now it felt strange and foreign to her; it had not merely changed, it had actually become a completely different kind of town. Still, she knew where she had to go first. She continued driving through town, down along the seaside road, toward the old Barlowe mansion.

She did half-expect Ellis's house to be gone, or in a shambles; or worse, converted into condominiums. To her relief, it still stood proudly overlooking the Atlantic, though now painted a somewhat garish combination of maroon, green and yellow. A large sign outside boasted: WAINSCOTT POINT INN: A VICTORIAN BED-AND-BREAKFAST.

Rose parked her truck and emerged warily, her eyes sweeping across the grounds. The simple plots she and Ellis had planted had been replaced by huge, exuberant Victorian period gardens, complete with treillage, topiary and pergolas. But by the far edge of the property, she was pleased to see a grouping of wildly overgrown yew and hemlock, the very bushes planted by Ellis himself so many years ago.

She climbed up the front steps, feeling only the faintest

sense of familiarity, nostalgia: It came, she thought, from the scent of salt air, the motion of coming up the steps and walking around the curve of porch. Where once she might have come upon Ellis, slumped in a chair, engrossed in Durant—slowly raising his gray-blue eyes to her—there were now only Victorian accessories and knickknacks, ferns in urns and cast-iron garden furniture.

A cheery, thirtyish woman in a denim jumper, with a cap of red-brown hair, bounded out onto the porch. "Hel-lo. Welcome to the Wainscott Point Inn. Have you a reservation?" she sang out, with a strong Southern accent.

"Well, no, but—"

"I'm *so* sorry. We have no vacancies, absolutely not a one. We're all booked up, what with Wainscott Days Festival, and all. Everyone is. But you might find something over on the mainland—"

"Actually, I just stopped to take a look at the house."

"Yes. Oh, yes. Isn't it gorgeous? My husband and I just finished restoring it, completely. We took it all the way back to Victorian, every detail, every board and shingle. We even have our very own ghost." She giggled. "Old man Barlowe, some nineteenth-century gent, I think, who got murdered here." She drew an imaginary sword across her throat and giggled again.

Rose, slightly shaken, rubbed her forehead. "Do you know anything about the family who lived here? The Barlowes?"

"Well, not much. The house was abandoned when we took over. But do you know, we had a Mr. Barlowe here just the other night, but I don't know if he had any connection to the house. Very quiet man, didn't say two words to us all the time he was here."

Rose discreetly grabbed the porch railing to steady herself. "Was he Ellis Barlowe?" she asked, calmly.

"No. His first name was . . . Let me think. Barlowe,

Barlowe . . . Oh, wait, I'll get the ledger." She motioned for Rose to follow her inside, where the interior was predictably furnished: brocade wallpaper, fringed lamps, lace curtains and roses everywhere. The innkeeper pointed to the fine, spidery, slightly backward signature in her visitors' book, a signature heartbreakingly familiar to Rose: Theo Barlowe. He gave, as his home address: Mount Benedetto, Pennsylvania. Rose touched the writing with one finger. According to the book, he'd been there only two nights before. While she was at Benedetto . . .

"This is the man . . . who used to own this house."

"Really!" The innkeeper squealed. "Boy, *that* explains a lot. He was just looking, looking, looking at everything. Just walking around and around the property and gardens. But he wouldn't talk to us, wouldn't come down for cocktails or breakfast. . . . We just thought he was really *odd*, but I guess he just couldn't get over what we'd done to the place."

I bet he couldn't, Rose thought.

"But it's funny, I heard all kinds of different rumors about this place, when we first came up from Atlanta," the woman went on, her brow wrinkling in an almost comic manner. "About the murder, yes, and the ghosts. But I also heard the last owner was a Catholic priest, who kept a sexy mistress up here." She giggled in a scandalous way, and Rose, too, had to restrain herself from laughing out loud.

"But how do *you* know Mr. Barlowe?"

"I was a . . . landscaper here, you might say. I helped him with his gardens."

"Oh! This place was completely overgrown when we got it, just a mess. And we found the *oddest* plants! Of course, we had to rip everything out, but we really wanted a period garden, completely Victorian, just like those old Barlowes would have had. Being in gardening yourself, I'm sure you understand all the work that went into it."

"Yes," Rose murmured. The woman seemed to be waiting

for praise, congratulations, but Rose decided she probably got enough from her paying guests. The garden was impressive, but too fussy for her taste.

"I'd just like to wander around a bit, could I?" she asked.

"Of course! I'm so sorry about us being filled up. I'm sure you'd love to stay a night, wouldn't you?"

"Another time." Rose glanced upward, at the ceiling. "That room, with the French doors and balcony, upstairs? What do you use that for?"

"You remember that room? Fabulous, isn't it! It's our honeymoon suite."

Rose wandered about the gardens and lawn, but there was nothing left to tug at her memory or spur thoughts of Ellis. Her mind was churning: He was here, but he's gone. Is he still in town? Back at the monastery? And where has he been the past two months? She glanced at her watch. Nearly 7 P.M., and she had nowhere to stay the night. And every hotel or motel in the area booked. It seemed to be a divine sign: Go home, Rose, give this up. Go back to your children, your husband.

"Hello? Hello! Mrs. Landscape Lady!" The owner of the inn came running out in her direction, her face pink with excitement.

"We *just* now had a cancellation, can you believe it! On a Saturday night, of all things! So we have a downstairs room, shared bath and of course full breakfast in the morning! Only ninety-five dollars. Would you want it?"

Rose, feeling faintly stunned, nodded. "Yes, fine. That'll be fine."

The room, as it turned out, was the old sunporch, the place she used to retreat to, to escape Ellis's dark moods. The big windows had been fitted with mauve miniblinds, and Rose rolled up each and every one to bring in the sky and sea. She went back into town, briefly—it was quieter now, a bit less crowded—and stalked up and down the streets, hoping feebly to spot Ellis somewhere: Somehow she was sure she had indeed seen him earlier, the tall, faceless man mingling into the summer crowds. But she had no luck.

She returned to the now-dark sunporch room, and carefully, slowly, dragged the small, single bed across the room until it was directly under the windows: This is where she had liked to sleep, whenever she'd been banished to this porch. She stretched out now and gazed up at the night sky, the bright crescent of moon directly overhead. She could almost sense Ellis silently creeping in, meek, contrite after bad words, a messy scene. Sliding into bed with her, struggling to fit his tall frame into the small bed, beside her.

I will love you forever, for eternity. Don't ever leave me. Yes, it was here, in this room, he spoke those words to her, whispering them in her ear. Her own private ghost. She shuddered: *No,* she thought. But could it be possible? Had Ellis returned to his home . . . to end his own life? "No, no," she whispered, trying to calm herself. No. Tomorrow, she thought, I'll find you, somehow.

17

ROSE vowed never to mention Burt Keating's name again, or to visit his farm. But one day she walked out onto the porch and found, at the top of the front stairs, an enormous plant, its pot wrapped in foil with a clumsy pink ribbon. She was still examining it when Ellis strolled out.

"What a . . . peculiar plant," he remarked, mystified. "What is it?"

"I'm not sure," she said, with a grin. "I think it's some kind of datura, 'Heaven's Trumpet.' I've only read about these, they plant them in South American graveyards. They blossom, like lilies, but only at night, and they're supposed to have this incredible fragrance, like incense—"

His face went pale. "Who would send us such a thing?"

"Someone aware, I suppose, of our interest in horticulture."

"Or someone wanting to mock my past."

"Oh, for goodness sake. I'm sure whoever sent it had no idea of its religious significance."

"Who sent it?"

"I have no idea." She did, but kept this knowledge to herself. She had no desire to provoke Ellis by mentioning Burt Keating's name. She brought the datura into the sun-room, which had become her own personal retreat from Ellis's dark moods. Here, wall-to-ceiling windows faced out over the sea, and the floor gleamed with cheerful Italian tiles; there was a daybed and plump furniture with uphol-stery bleached white by the sun. The datura seemed right at home here, safe from unpredictable Maine sea breezes.

A few days later, Ellis walked into the kitchen with a large, oblong white box in his arms. He silently laid it in front of her, then stood expectantly, arms folded. She looked at the box, then at his face: His gray eyes were blank, revealing nothing. Puzzled, she opened the box, peeling aside layers of tissue: The sweet, dizzying fragrance of roses wafted up from the tissue, and she carefully pulled out a huge, thorny bouquet of buds and blossoms in a spectrum of reds, from creamy pink to crimson.

"Ellis," she murmured. "They're beautiful. But—" she stopped, silenced by the icy look on his face.

"Who sent them?" he demanded in a low voice.

"I don't know. Maybe it's a mistake—"

He ripped a note off the box and threw it at her: It simply said, "To Mrs. Connolly: Roses for a Rose."

"A secret admirer," he continued, his voice trembling. "Someone you've been sneaking off to meet, someone else you're fucking, while I'm asleep—"

"Stop it!" she shouted. "Don't be ridiculous! There's no other man! It's preposterous!"

"Then who's sending you these goddamn flowers?" He gave the box a rough shove, sending it flying into her. She caught it and cradled it, protectively, in her arms.

"It's . . . it's just that silly Burt Keating, the nurseryman.

He seems to have developed a crush on me. Dear God, Ellis, do you think I'd actually prefer him to you?"

"How is it that my cousin would have the chance, the opportunity, to develop a crush on you? Have you been visiting him, chatting with him? Encouraging him—"

"No! No, no, no. Ellis, this is ridiculous. Look." She dumped the roses into a trash pail. "See. That's the end of it. Okay?"

But he didn't seem mollified in the least. "You're teasing me, taunting me. Why? What do you want from me?"

She was mystified. "What are you talking about?"

"You don't really love me at all, do you?"

"Stop this, Ellis. Please." She felt truly alarmed now, concerned about Ellis, his face contorted by some strange, secret rage that had nothing to do with roses or his cousin. Not ordinary jealousy, she thought, but something more primitive or visceral. She went to him now, to touch him: Usually that soothed him, her hands on his chest, her face against his, but this time he brushed by her and stalked off. She was unable to find him for the rest of the day.

Later that evening, he strolled casually toward her on the porch, as if nothing had happened.

"I've been out, looking at the green and yellow beans. I think they'll be ready soon for harvest."

She was sitting bent over her sketch pad, pen in hand: She lifted her eyes to him, warily, waiting a moment before answering. "Yes."

"Our first harvest. The first fruits of our labor."

She stared at him. He was working hard at making simple conversation, his voice almost tremulous; she heard the strain under the careful, precise statements he was making.

"You aren't thinking of leaving, are you?" he asked her.

"I think sometimes you're trying to drive me away."

"No, no." His eyes glistened. "I am sorry, Rose. I didn't know I had a jealous streak. I've never really been in love before. I don't know how to act properly."

"You must have loved someone else, at some time. You're not a young man, there must have been someone—"

"That's what makes it so pathetic. A man my age, just learning to love, now . . ."

"But you've had other women, you said . . ."

"Oh, yes. Dozens. Before seminary, before the priesthood. Dozens, but not one face or name lingers in my memory. I may have thought I was in love with one girl or another, but it would only be some brief infatuation. Not like this, Rose. Nothing like this."

"Women," she murmured, without thinking. "But no men."

Ellis, aghast, fell backward against the porch railing. "*No!*" he snapped. "I'm not the least bit homosexual! Why would you even mention that?"

"I wasn't implying that you were. It was a stupid thing to say."

"You see that in me, don't you?"

"No, no."

"You wouldn't be the first to do so."

"I know—"

"You *know*?!"

"About Graham Keating—"

Ellis flushed in outrage. "Yes, I suppose your friend Burt told you about that."

"I asked him about it. How your nose came to be broken. I'm sorry," she added, meekly, watching him struggling to contain himself, to control his temper. He hurtled about the porch, pacing, brushing his hair back, but when he wheeled back around, his face was melancholy, but calm.

"He would be a better man for you, wouldn't he? Burt? A better husband."

"I don't want him," she whispered. "It's you I want."

"Seems that everyone leaves me eventually. Why should you be any different?"

"I'm not going to leave you. How can I convince you of that?"

"You can't," he said, softly. "I'm a born doubter. I lack faith."

"Was that why you left the priesthood?"

He considered this, his eyes dropping to the floor of the porch. "Maybe. I'm exhausted, Rose. Not physically, but inside. A priest needs inner resources, something to draw on. Faith, grace, inner strength, unfaltering devotion, energy for God's work. There was nothing left by the time I got to St. Cyril's. I was like a boat with a small leak. With each parish, I just kept taking on more and more water. I'm sunk now, I think."

"Don't say that."

"I've come to see my entire priestly career as a sham, a worthless act. Just a desperate attempt to give meaning to my wretched life. I doubt that I ever had any true vocation. So how can I go back to something I never should have been involved with in the first place?"

"You can't," she said in barely a whisper. "Oh, Ellis. Are you thinking of returning?"

"But I can't, can I? Not now. That's the frightening thing about falling in love with you."

She swallowed. "I don't think . . . you were meant to be a priest. You didn't make a bad choice. But now . . . you just have to figure out what to do next."

He held out his hands to her in a despairing, beseeching gesture, then let them drop to his thighs.

"I don't *know*, Ellis. Perhaps you think too much. Perhaps you should simply try to find a job somewhere. Something else to fill up your time."

"Sure. Maybe I'll open up a nursery."

She winced at the snideness in his voice and gave him a push. "Go for a walk. You always say that helps you think. Walk all the way around the island if you have to, but something will come to you, I'm sure of it. Go on, go."

He made his way down the steps, mutely, obediently, turning to her a few yards away. His face was a plea; his voice plaintive: "You don't really have any feelings for him, do you?"

"No, Ellis. *No.*"

He seemed momentarily relieved. But down by the surf, he stopped to turn once more, worriedly, in her direction. He continued down along the edge of the water with a halting, uncertain step.

18

L UCAS flopped about the big double bed in Rose's guest room, unable to get comfortable, unable to drift off to sleep. It was an incredibly humid night, sticky, and the small room seemed stifling, airless. He got up and tried to force open the room's one window as far as it would go, then stood, watching mosquitoes and other bugs slap themselves up against the screen. There was the shrill din of crickets and the muted roar of a distant highway; he saw lights on the ridge beyond Rose's fields. A different countryside than Benedetto, and suddenly he felt a startling wave of . . . was it *home*sickness for Benedetto? How odd, he thought, that he should be here, in his native state, less than fifty miles from his birthplace, yet yearn for a "home" hundreds of miles away. And yet he did have an unmistakable yearning to be back in his narrow little cot in his cool, quiet cell at Benedetto, with its window that overlooked the mountains of Pennsylvania and West Virginia.

He stood in the darkness for a while, waiting vainly for

a breeze, and soon Amanda's voice hit his ears: hushed, far away, earnest talking. She was on the phone, he guessed— Rose?—and he shut his eyes, struggling to hear her words.

". . . he's there? He's actually up there, in Maine?"

Had she said that, or had he merely imagined it? He grabbed his pants and struggled into them, then emerged, hesitantly, from his room, rubbing his eyes against the light of the hall. He saw Amanda, slouched up against the kitchen doorway, the phone receiver pressed to her ear. She grinned when she saw him, but suddenly turned away from him.

"Thanks, Uncle Graham. Hope your leg is better. And if you see Mom . . . if you happen to see her, tell her to call me."

"Theo is in Maine?" Lucas managed to ask.

Amanda hung up the phone with a brisk slam, then regarded him in a way that seemed both curious and imperious. He felt uncomfortably aware of her eyes on his naked chest—which despite his thinning head of hair was covered in unruly dark fur.

"Were you eavesdropping? That's not very monklike."

"I overheard by accident," he protested. "And for your information, eavesdropping is very monklike. It's practically a tradition at Benedetto."

"I'm sure you have many interesting traditions up there," she remarked, drily.

"What did your uncle have to say?"

"Apparently your Theo is there. Or was there. Graham didn't make it very clear, he's really out of it, unfortunately. You know, senile. But he did seem to know what I was talking about. He kept talking about 'Ellis Barlowe's grand return,' so I'm pretty sure your Theo was there. Maybe still is."

"But you haven't heard from Rose."

Now a worried, vaguely hurt expression crossed Amanda's face. "No. It's not like Mom to do that. Not call, or let us know where she is. Where she's spending the night." Her voice dropped. "Who knows. Perhaps she's with him now."

"Or maybe on her way back here," offered Lucas.

"That's possible, isn't it?" She began walking toward him. "It's late, very late, Mr. Monk, and if you're going to help with chores, you have to be up with the sun. But first"— she hooked a slender finger into the waistband of his pants—"you better take these off. I have to—" She burst into delighted, raucous laughter at the shock in his face. "I have to do a load of laundry, so go, get me that sweater, too."

He retrieved it and handed it to her humbly, embarrassed: He hadn't quite realized how grungy it was, reeking still of the mothballs it was kept in at Benedetto, along with everyone else's worldly clothes.

"I'll slip the pants out later," he murmured. But as she took the sweater from him her fingers grazed his chest, then lingered there, and he felt another wave of unexpected physical desire, mingled now with intense curiosity about her, the body beneath her thin calico dress. If he kissed her, would it be like kissing Theo? Their mouths were the exact same shape. Her eyes glowed back at him: Challenging? Teasing? Mocking? Beckoning? He couldn't tell.

Her hand remained on his chest, and now she pushed him backward, lightly, with the tips of her fingers. "Go on, go back to sleep. We'll hear about my other father some other day."

19

ROSE woke the following morning—crisp early sunlight poured through the tall windows of the sunporch, the sky almost painfully blue—feeling suprisingly, and bitterly, depressed. She was struck with the utter folly, the stupidity of her actions: driving, on a whim, first to western Pennsylvania, then up to Maine, while her husband literally lay dying. Driving up here like a maniac, as if she had some plan, some specific idea where she'd find Ellis.

Logic told her that he was probably gone: He'd probably spent one perverse, curious night here, in his former home, and was perhaps making his way back to Benedetto . . .

She pulled herself out of bed and decided to skip the lavish breakfast that came with her stay. In the parlor, she made a discreet phone call, dialing the number of Mount Benedetto Abbey.

"I need to speak with Father Theophane Barlowe," she asked, in a tremulous whisper. "I'm sorry," said the smooth, male voice on the other end of the line. "Father has not returned from his trip, though we expect him sometime this week."

She set the receiver down, not sure what to make of this. She then slipped outside into the still-cool Sunday morning air and began walking toward town. It was less than a mile, as she recalled, and she hoped the walk would soothe her, give her a chance to think.

It occurred to her that Ellis might have checked in with the Catholic pastor here in Wainscott as a courtesy; perhaps he was even staying at the rectory. She decided she would talk with the local priest, after Mass, and followed the others into the old, ornate brownstone building.

She felt some trepidation: It had been more than thirty years since she'd set foot in a Catholic Church, or any church, except for Amanda's ill-fated wedding in Wisterville's Episcopal Church. Now she slid into the back pew, feeling overwhelmed with emotion: a sense of guilty regret, sadness, a powerful sense of nostalgia, even longing. Her eyes swept greedily over the vaulted ceilings, the stained-glass gleaming jewel-like against the morning sky. It was so different now: The Mass was in English, and the priest faced forward, wearing simpler vestments. She recited, numbly, without thinking, the words of the Kyrie, the Gloria, the ancient prayers she'd learned as a girl, in Latin.

The youngish priest stepped forward. "We have a special speaker today, for the homily. An amazing man, an amazing priest, a former resident of Wainscott who now has a special mission in Pennsylvania, working with the terminally ill and sufferers of the AIDS virus. We'll be having a second collection today to benefit his work there. Please welcome Father Theophane Barlowe."

Rose, sitting perfectly still, felt herself grow dizzy, her face flushed. Her heart pounded dangerously, and she laid a hand over her breast, as if to still it, silence it, her eyes now focused on the tall, slender silver-haired man who emerged from the sacristy. Dressed in the graceful, flowing white-and-gray robes of Mount Benedetto, the sleeves pushed up to his elbows, sandaled feet slapping against the marble floors, he walked swiftly, confidently, as if he were in a hurry to begin speaking. Rose had not known what to expect at all: Here was a man whose body she had known intimately, and yet had not seen in thirty years. A man past seventy: She could not guess if he'd be frail and sickly, or awkwardly heavy as some slim young men often become. She half-expected a grizzled, bearded old hermit. But she saw a man who could easily pass for fifty or sixty, yet a man she instantly recognized as *her* Ellis, with the same noble profile, clean-shaven, gray-blue eyes (now behind wire-rimmed glasses), even the same sweep of hair falling carelessly over his brow, though it was white, no longer blond.

And yet, there was something profoundly different about him. Something she had been unable to pick up in their long, careful, tiptoe correspondence with each other. She leaned forward, watching him, as he made his way down into the middle of the aisle in a relaxed, oddly friendly way. He actually smiled at the congregation.

"Let me begin by talking about an intensely complicated issue, one that affects all of us eventually. Of course, I mean death. Technology has forced us to think hard about it, to think hard about the quality of our lives, the wisdom of prolonging life or of hastening death itself. And so often what's missing in this debate are spiritual considerations . . ."

Despite his rather somber subject, he seemed amazingly warm, animated; she was reminded, faintly, of his old adult education lectures, when she'd first become fascinated with him. It struck her that he was not a troubled man at all, and she felt disoriented, confused, surprisingly dismayed and disappointed. Why had she such a strong sense that he was in trouble? Her scenario called for a dispirited, despondent Ellis, desperately in need of her comfort and consolation. And yet the Ellis that had materialized was calm, exuding an unmistakable sort of inner glow, or peace. She could see it reflected in the faces of the churchgoers who watched him avidly, and with interest.

". . . at Benedetto, we try to provide a gateway, a gracious portal into the hereafter, an appropriate transition between life and union with the Father, and we strive to make this journey as peaceful, as meaningful, as blessed and comfortable as possible . . ."

I should be happy for him, she thought: He is alive, he is well. He seems happy, content. And yet she felt nothing but a stinging sense of sorrow and loss, combined with an odd sense of humiliation. Her eyes filled with tears as she watched him turn and retreat back up onto the altar, slipping out the way he came in.

But she encountered him again as she emerged from Mass: He was standing at the foot of the steps with the local priest, greeting people who'd been impressed, or moved, by his talk. They pressed money into his hands, bills that he accepted in a grateful but vaguely embarrassed way. She stood off to one side, wondering how to approach him. She wished the crowd about him would dissipate, but a new crowd of worshipers was arriving for the next Mass. She took her place in line with the others.

And finally, there he was, before her. He was in the process of awkwardly trying to fold a twenty-dollar bill and glanced up at her in a bland, expectant way. His eyes were utterly blank, and she saw only the mildest interest in his face, as if she were just another churchgoer from an unfamiliar parish.

It was too much for her: She turned and fled. She walked, and kept walking, not allowing the tears to flow until she was well beyond the limits of the town, back on a lonely stretch of road. She hurried back into the house before anyone could spot her, and barricaded herself in her room, the old sunporch.

She took a small hand mirror from the dresser and examined her face, which was blotchy with emotion. Yes, she was old now, but surely not so unrecognizable? Her hair was grayer and shorter, her face a little worse for wear, but there was still enough of the old Rose in her, she thought, for Ellis to remember her, if he chose to. Her eyes, the shape of her face, the shape of her mouth . . .

It's not *me*, she thought, an awful awareness crashing now into her brain. It's him: his mind. It must be going. Surely, she thought, a form of senility that allowed him to function efficiently enough in the present, but had robbed him of his memories, perhaps his entire past. That summer, their love, those months, those moments were lost to him now, perhaps: He was truly Theophane the monk now, all traces of tortured Ellis gone, with no recollection of his "before" life, the world that happened before Benedetto.

And perhaps that was why he'd begged his abbot to make this trip: to try to remember something that was, perhaps, nagging or poking at him, something just out of the reach of his memory. Should I go back, she wondered: seek him out and force him to remember? Or was it better, more merciful, to simply let him be, and keep the past undisturbed?

There was a brisk knock at the door. She jumped and cracked it open, hesitantly. Hopefully . . . But it was only the husband-innkeeper, as cheerful and effervescent as his wife.

"Hey there, Mrs. Keating. We missed you at breakfast this morning."

"I'm sorry," she murmured, her hand still on the door, ready to shut him out.

"You've got a visitor. There's an old gent out in the parlor, wanting to see you." He winked. "Says he's an old, old friend of yours."

20

BURT'S gifts continued to arrive, almost on a daily basis. She would go out to the front porch and find something there, waiting for her: a huge bunch of freshly cut peonies, a small flat box of raspberries, a potted pepper plant with a full and abundant bloom of yellow and orange spears, a small burlap sack filled with tender, tiny round new potatoes.

Rose understood what was happening: Burt was indeed courting her, in a gentle but relentless way. She felt perplexed, fearful of Ellis's reaction—she had to hide everything from him—but secretly flattered, warmed by the nurseryman's affection. But she knew she had to discourage him, somehow, gently; she really had no room in her heart for anyone else but Ellis, however troubled and troubling he might be.

"You must stop sending me gifts," she finally told Burt. They were standing in his blueberry patch, picking tiny, dusky berries. Burt grabbed a fistful and threw them into her carton.

"Ain't no real harm in it, is there?" He glanced back at her. "You're not really serious about Barlowe, are you?"

"I am. God help me, but I am."

He shrugged, as if this mattered little to him.

"Can't last, Rose. I don't think Barlowe's the marrying kind. Anyways, he's still a priest, ain't he?"

She merely sighed and plucked a few more berries from the bush.

"Don't see any ring around your finger."

She looked down at her own weatherbeaten hands, the raised purplish veins signaling, she thought, the start of middle age.

"What do you suppose Mr. Barlowe would do," Burt continued, "if I were to buy you a ring?"

"Oh, Burt," she whispered. "Please don't."

He tossed another handful of berries into the basket, crushing most of them, she noticed: He seemed to be growing increasingly agitated. "Just a thought. You're way too good for him. A strong, handsome girl like you needs a husband. Someone decent, respectable. Strong. Strong in body, but in mind, too." He paused. "I worry about you, Rose. I worry about you every day, alone with him, in that big house."

Rose glanced over at him, perplexed. "Whatever for?" To her utter alarm, Burt suddenly threw down the bucket he'd been holding, berries exploding out all over them both.

"He *killed* his father! The man killed his own father, what's to say he won't kill you, too?"

Rose stared at him, stunned beyond belief.

"You said . . . it was a suicide."

"That's what the newspapers said. The police. But *I* know, Rose. I heard him say it, with my own ears. I ran into him, on the beach—afterward. After it happened. He was talking to himself, crying, I grabbed him by the shoulders. He kept saying, over and over, *he's dead, he's dead, I killed him. I* brought him to the police, Rose. Drove him there myself. But they let him off, I don't know why."

"You're lying," Rose snapped.

"I wish I were," he moaned.

"It can't be true. It can't be—" The image of the bed and its sinister stains popped into her head. "A man like Ellis isn't capable of killing . . ." But she could not forget the image of that bed. She ran from him, ran to her truck, jumped in and tore off down the road, back to the house she shared with Ellis.

She bounded up the stairs and rushed past him on the porch, hurtling through the house, upstairs, ripping away the boards, running down the hallway. She snatched the bloodied coverlet from the bed at the end of the hall and walked more calmly back downstairs with it bunched in her arms, out onto the porch, the stains seeming black in the bright afternoon sun.

She let it fall onto his feet. He did not seem to recognize it, staring down at it with mild confusion. Suddenly he cried and leapt from his chair, covering his mouth as if he might suddenly vomit.

"Are you a murderer?" she asked him, softly. "Can you explain this to me?"

He wrenched his face away from it. "Take it away, first. I can't . . . look at it . . ."

She gathered it up and brought it over to the trash bin. When she returned, she was startled to see him sitting calmly in his chair, waiting for her. But he was still very pale, as if he might pass out.

"I was going to tell you, Rose. Everything. I was just rehearsing it all in my mind, trying to put it together in a coherent way. In a way that wouldn't scare you—"

"Hearing the rumors, seeing this bed was more frightening than anything you could have told me."

"I know that, now. But it's so hard to speak of." His voice was barely a whisper. "I've never talked about this, not even to a confessor, no one. I haven't been able to."

"You killed your father."

"No. I didn't, not intentionally. It was an accident." He folded his arms together, hugging himself. "But they say there are no such things as accidents. So perhaps I did mean to kill him. I certainly had reason to."

"Why? What reason could you possibly have to kill your own father?"

He froze, seeming unwilling to go on. "My father was . . . a brilliant man, a brilliant doctor. But not right in the head. He didn't really know how to behave with people. He was either cold and unpleasant with them, or . . . inappropriate."

"Inappropriate? What does that mean?"

"In his clinic, they said he touched people—well, children, young people mostly, in an . . . indecent manner. He was . . . sexual with them." And now he bent forward, burying his head in his hands. Suddenly Rose understood.

"And with you, too," she whispered.

"He was like two different men. I never knew what man to expect. And sometimes I put up with it, sometimes I fought him. He was my father: You're supposed to love and respect your father, especially if he's this great healer. But I knew, I knew what a filthy, false man he really was." He raised his head. "When he became ill, with that awful cancer, it seemed *just*. It seemed to me, as a young, tentative, secret Catholic, proper punishment from the Almighty. It was like my prayers had been answered. I wanted him to die, I *wanted* him to suffer! I missed the really important lesson of Catholicism: redemption and forgiveness."

"How can you forgive the unforgivable?"

"I don't know. I know now that no one should have to go through what he went through before he died. He was in hellish pain, constant, unrelenting. And it went on, and on, and on. He was a stubborn, proud man, so he didn't want anyone to know, none of his colleagues, what was happening to him. He made me bring him back here. And I had to take care of him. Whether I wanted to or not. The odd thing is that despite all the pain and agony he was in, not once did he ask me to help him end it all. Later, as a priest, I actually got requests for that from dying strangers. But my father did not want to die. I think he actually believed, irrationally, toward the end, that he was going to survive and recover. So I don't even have the consolation of believing I'd fulfilled his final wish."

"How did it happen? How do you accidentally kill someone?"

"I gave him too much morphine one night. He'd had a particularly bad day, very bad, and I was thinking . . . if I gave him just a little more than usual, it might put him to sleep or into some kind of restful coma for a while. I must have been mad myself to think such a thing, that a seventeen-year-old boy could determine a nonlethal dose of morphine. He never woke up. In the morning, he was dead."

"And you told Burt. And the police came—"

"I don't remember any of that. I can't remember anything after finding my father's cold body in that bed. My grandfather came and got me off somehow. I do remember him talking with the police, the coroner, telling them about my father's cancer, even making up some absurd story about my father planning his own suicide. My grandfather got me off and brought me back here and helped me to get ready to go off to Dartmouth. As if nothing had happened. But I knew, in the way he spoke to me, looked at me, regarded me, that he'd judged me guilty. He believed I'd intentionally killed his son. And he did not approve of me at all."

"Morphine," Rose murmured. "But that's not a bloody way to die."

"That wasn't my father's blood on the bed, Rose."

Rose tensed, waiting for more.

"The night before I was to leave for Dartmouth, I went up to my father's room. I didn't want to go away to college. I didn't know what I wanted to do. I wanted to grieve for my father and felt I had no right to, no basis for it. Wasn't he a monstrous sort of man, cold one moment, molesting me the next, forcing me into a kind of slave labor when he became ill? Yet I missed him for some strange reason. I missed him, and I'd been responsible for his death. I couldn't make sense of it all. And when I got upstairs, and was in his room, and lay down on his bed, the bed where he'd died, I realized the deepest truth of all: that I no longer wanted to be in this world. That I could not bear to live another second more. And the only thing I could find was my father's old razor." And now he showed Rose his wrists, the faint pink stigmata there. "I wasn't insane, Rose. I don't want you to think that. I only faltered, that one time—"

"Someone found you."

"Yes. Old Grandfather Barlowe. He was not pleased. Not pleased at all by what he called my 'stunt.' To him, psychology and mental sickness was a superstition; he didn't believe in it. He didn't even take me to the hospital, but had a local doctor called in secretly to stitch me up. And just a few days later, he put me on that train, bandages and all, to Dartmouth."

"Oh, Ellis. Oh, Ellis." She went to him now, embracing him tightly. He seemed amazed.

"This doesn't horrify you, appall you?"

"No, no. I can see why it was hard to tell me. But you did tell me, and it's not so bad, not so bad as I imagined. All this time, I thought you were just running away from being a priest. But these secrets! How could you hold them in so long? It's amazing that you're still—" She almost said *sane*, but had bitten her tongue just in time. Of course he's sane, she told herself.

"I still feel so imperfect," he murmured, closing his eyes. "Faulty, not worthy of you. Or your love."

"Ellis, listen. I have my own secrets. Things I didn't tell you, because I was afraid, too. Of losing you."

He opened his eyes, in wonder.

"I was pregnant, once. Shortly after I married my husband. I had just realized what sort of man I'd married, a moody man with a vicious temper, abusive . . . I panicked, went down to New York City on the train—a neighbor told me where to go—and I got rid of it." She paused. "I just didn't want it then. Under the circumstances. Even now, to be truthful, I don't feel much remorse about it. Maybe that's my sin."

"That's an excommunicative offense, Rose. Abortion."

She nodded. "I know. I confessed it. And I was absolved. But I paid dearly for it, I had my penance. I contracted an infection and nearly died, nearly bled to death. And then the doctors told me I would be sterile forever. Proper punishment, I suppose, for dealing with an inconvenient child. For marrying a man I didn't love for his money, his property, his farm, security. Then a second penance, when he went crazy. He didn't leave a suicide note, but if he had, I know he would have blamed me, he would've said I drove him to it—" She began to sob, and felt his fingers touching her face, her hair. "Don't, Rose, don't," he crooned softly, pulling her tightly against him.

"But what I'm telling you is, you and I, we're on equal footing, Ellis. Unhappy pasts, secrets . . . uncertain futures."

"Yes, yes," he whispered, his eyes lighting up in an odd, beatific way. "We *are* alike. I've always sensed it. We're kindred souls, tortured souls, created for each other." His embrace tightened. "Rose, we must leave here."

"I'll go wherever you go."

"Will you?" His voice was tremulous, filled with a child-like sort of joy.

"Of course. I'll never leave you, Ellis, never."

"Then we must go. We will go," he said in a calm, decisive way.

21

AMANDA, still clad in her nightgown, opened up the blinds of the guest bedroom, letting in the late-morning sunlight. She regarded with amusement the naked, soundly sleeping monk, or ex-monk, lying diagonally across the messy, rumpled bed. She wasn't entirely sure he was completely naked, since the top sheet was wound tightly about his torso and thighs. But it was evident that he'd had a restless, active, perhaps fretful sort of night.

She placed on a bedside chair his sweater and jeans, straight from the dryer and wondered how to broach the more delicate task of persuading him to shower or bathe. Not that he really reeked, yet—Amanda was not especially offended by odors, and in certain men actually found sweat an erotic stimulant—but she thought he ought to be clean and fresh for his reentry into the world, if that was what he had in mind.

"Luke? Hey, Lukey boy." She shook him, but he was out cold, dead to the world. She pulled at the top sheet and saw that he was indeed wearing underwear—big old yellow-gray boxer shorts that looked as if he'd swiped them from some ancient monk. She clucked her tongue and went off to pluck a spare pair from Tommy's drawer. Her little brother favored child-bright colors and patterns, so she selected snug jockeys in purple-and-orange tiger stripes and grinned: Wait till he wakes up and finds himself in these, she thought with delight.

On the way back to the guest room, she glanced at the clock. Just before 11 A.M.: She no longer attended church, but Hank had taken Tommy earlier in the morning. Now both brothers were out in the cornfields; the nursery's retail shop would open at noon. Everyone would be coming in for the corn: rooting through the bins and peeling back the husks and throwing them back in and demanding to know why the yellow corn wasn't separated from the white . . . She was tempted to simply put a sign in the window: GO AWAY. Or, CLOSED: DUE TO FAMILY TRAGEDY. Tragedies. A dying father and crazy mother.

But she did feel herself softening up, grudgingly, reluctantly, toward Rose. She wanted to stay mad and upset with her, but the adult woman inside wouldn't let her: She'd finally identified the real emotion she felt in regard to Rose's whole endeavor. It was jealousy, pure and simple. It wasn't fair that her dowdy, sixtyish, old mom should be embarking on this breathless, achingly romantic adventure, while she, Amanda, young and firm and antsy, should be stuck on the farm with no prospects, no lost love in her own brief past. Moreover, Rose had upset all of Amanda's own conclusions about men and love: that there was no perfect man, no perfect love, and there probably wasn't much sense in bothering to look for either.

I'd love it if I were wrong, she thought with a sigh. If I met a man tomorrow who set me melting, all aquiver, with love and passion. Not likely, however. She reentered Lucas's room, twirling Tommy's underwear on her finger, feeling itchy and bored and frustrated all at once.

She tugged off his top sheet. He was lying on his side, his back to her, so she began pulling the old boxers down over his buttocks—which were surprisingly cute, she noted with a smile, tight and firm. But there was some resistance from up front. The shorts were stuck on something. She peered over him and nearly whooped with laughter at the size of his erection.

She carefully rolled him onto his back, so she could really get a look at it. Yes, she thought, certainly impressive for such a small guy, really. It had that same taut, tight, *new* quality that teenage boys' erections had, and she had to squeeze her fingers up into tight fists to keep from touching it.

No, she told herself, absolutely not! The look on his face, meanwhile, was positively angelic, even calm, under the faintly rakish two-day growth of beard. Yet she placed her hands on his thighs, almost experimentally. Thighs which were, like the rest of his somewhat slight, stubby body, pleasingly hairy, lots of soft dark fine hair, a vaguely feral-like quality Amanda always enjoyed in a man. She caressed his thighs lightly and his penis quivered in a hopeful way. She stroked around and around, but not touching; and heard his breath coming a little quicker.

Evil woman, she told herself, growing flushed and bothered herself, an achy kind of pleasure creeping in between her own legs. Seducing a poor, pure, defenseless monk. But she felt rather desperate herself: She too had been celibate for a while, ever since coming back under Rose's roof. And here was this splendid hard-on, this wonderful erection, going to waste.

I can't, she thought: It would be like raping him! Certainly taking unfair advantage, though he'd probably love it . . . She guessed he was a virgin, and this excited her even more: No other person has touched *this*, she thought, letting her fingers close in around it. She bent over and slid her tongue up the side of it, to the top and around, and he emitted a soft, sleepy low groan.

"I can't stand it," she murmured. She tugged off her own nightdress and climbed up onto him, straddling his body with her thighs. Still clutching his penis in her hand, she pressed her face against his.

"Lucas?" she whispered, breathless. "Luke, wake up. Do you want it? Do you?"

"Oh," he merely murmured, his eyes still shut tightly.

"Do you? Do you?"

"Yes, yes . . ."

She let him slip and slide right into her—she was more than ready—and then rocked her hips, feeling her own desire taking shape, suspecting he was going to come swiftly by the way he was breathing, the contortions of his face, the way he was now actually thrusting up, into her . . . She was just on the edge, when suddenly he stopped, with a great, surprised "Oh!" and she felt his organ contracting inside her.

"Theo," he gasped. "Oh, oh, Theo."

She froze, her desire instantly slipping away. His hands were reaching out now, first resting on her abdomen, then sliding up to her breasts, where they stopped suddenly. His eyes flew open.

"Oh, my God," he whispered. "Oh, God." He pulled his hands away, as if they'd been burned.

Amanda climbed off him, imperiously. Men had called her other names before, in the heat of sex—"Janet" or "Alice," which had disturbed her faintly—but no one had ever called her by a *man's* name before. And certainly not the assumed name of her biological father.

"I get it now," she snapped. "You and Barlowe were *fucking* each other up there. You thought *I* was *him*?!"

149

"No, no! *No!*" he sputtered, blinking furiously, probably still trying to awaken himself. "We never . . . we never did that!" He grabbed the sheet frantically. "What . . . what were you doing to me?!"

"But you were thinking about him. You're *sick!*" she shouted, picking up the tiger-striped underpants and flinging them in his face.

22

"First thing I'm going to do," Ellis told her, carrying an enormous stack of thick books, "is get rid of these."

It was the stack of Durant books he'd been making his way through all summer. She frowned.

"Have you read them all?"

"Of course not. But I've read enough. I'm sick of it, all that wretched human history. I don't need it. I don't want it cluttering my brain anymore."

They drove through town onto the bridge to the mainland. She thought perhaps he was taking her to Portland, when he abruptly stopped on the bridge. He leaped out of the truck, then started flinging the volumes of Durant over the bridge into the water, with startling venom.

"Ellis!" Alarmed, she tried to stop him, but he snatched the rest of the books out of her reach and deposited them into the muddy, swirling, algae-choked waters under the old wooden bridge.

"Why did you feel the need to do that?"

He responded with a haughty shrug, then backed the truck over the bridge, and drove back to his house.

"Have you given any thought," she asked him, a bit more meekly, "to where we'll be going when we leave here?"

"I haven't worked it out yet, Rose," he replied in a soft but impatient, vaguely irritated way.

"But what about your house? All this stuff?"

"I don't really care about it anymore. I think we should just leave it here, and let someone come and take it over."

"It doesn't work that way, Ellis. What'll happen is the government or someone will step in and take it. You should think about putting the house on the market . . ." She trailed off, seeing his face tighten in a dangerous way. "All right, all right. But let me at least clean it before we leave."

She was thinking about the mattress that still remained in Ellis's father's room; it was as chillingly stained as the bedspread had been. Ellis was remarkably calm when helping her remove it: They pulled it across the room and hoisted it over the balcony to be disposed of later on. Ellis then turned his attention to the bookcases.

"This was my father's great love. These damn books. Collecting them, acquiring them, hoarding them up here . . . What was the point of it all?" He began touching them, fingering the bindings in an almost tender way. Then abruptly, he began yanking them off the shelves, flinging them onto the floor. He cleared the shelves with quick, angry gestures, kicking aside the volumes that fell into his path. When he was done, he stared at the heap of books and pages scattered across the floor in a calm but contemptuous way.

"Are you going to throw those into the bay, too?"

"No, no. Call that vulture Edna. Let her bloody collector have them, if he's so eager for them. In fact"—he wandered out into the hallway, his mood oddly brighter—"we'll get rid of everything. Let Edna have it all. Yes, yes. And we'll sell the house, too. You are right, Rose, you are so splendidly practical. We'll get rid of all this junk, and this house, and maybe, then . . ." She saw the bitterness fall away from his face, replaced by a wan, hopeful look. Impulsively she went to him, hugged him tightly. He did not resist or pull away.

"We'll be free," she told him, joyfully.

"You handle it, Rose," he whispered. "I can't."

"I will," she murmured, feeling some of her own sickness and distress lift. "Everything will be fine."

Edna was euphoric. To Rose's dismay, she decided that the Barlowe furniture should be auctioned off: a grand, day-long event on the grounds of the estate, wooden chairs under a striped tent, tea and refreshments on the porch. "Some of your herbal teas," she murmured to Rose, "would be just charming."

Rose threw up her hands. "Just do your job. I don't want anything to do with this circus." Then, to Ellis: "Are we selling *everything?*"

"Everything," he said stubbornly, his eyes going down the annotated list Edna had prepared after a careful inspection of the entire upstairs and downstairs, attic and cellar. "Just leave our bed where it is until the day of the auction. That's all we need."

The auction was set for the following Saturday. Edna posted notices around town and ran blocky ads in the society section of the local newspaper:

A Once-in-a-Lifetime Event!

Auction of Magnificent Antique Furnishings from the 18th-c. Barlowe Estate, Spanning Three Centuries. Antiques, furniture, china, pewter, silver, fine art, Oriental rugs. Viewing begins at 8 A.M.; auction will begin promptly at 10!!

Within days, curious people came to the front door asking for a sneak peek; Rose sent them away impatiently but saw others lurking about the property, peering in the windows, even in the evening, when she and Ellis were preparing for bed.

"We've become celebrities," he remarked drily. He seemed oddly calm, even amused by the whole idea.

"Ellis, what are we going to do after the auction? Where will we go?"

"Don't worry. I'll tell you, when the time comes."

"I hate surprises," she told him. But he moved away from her, clearly preoccupied with whatever plans he'd secretly made. A little later, they came together in bed. Sex in late August was less frequent than in the days of early summer, but she was still grateful for it, nonetheless. But on this night, Ellis could not complete the act: He endlessly thrust into her, finally withdrawing with a disgusted sigh and flopping onto his side of the bed without saying a word to her. She was disconcerted, unable to understand what this was about.

On Thursday, men arrived to move the larger pieces of furniture into the barn until Saturday morning. Ellis, slung over the railing of the porch, watched them idly: To Rose's dismay, he'd begun smoking again, though he did not do so in her presence. But she saw the curl of smoke rising up from his hands, the discarded butts at his feet and even in the soil around the herb plants he'd once tended so carefully.

That day, too, the real-estate agent Edna had recommended arrived, a rather frantic, worried middle-aged woman wearing a wool suit despite the heat of summer. Ellis pushed her off on Rose. She surveyed the house with anxious eyes, wringing her hands, pointing out defects Rose had never noticed before. She did let Rose know, however, that several people had already expressed interest in the house, and asked if she could bring them by immediately.

"Please," Rose pleaded. "Can't we wait until after the auction?"

The woman looked alarmed. "You won't be here, will you? I mean, where will you and Father Barlowe—Oh!" She blushed deeply at her gaffe. "I mean, *Mister* Barlowe, of course. Where will you go? To Portland? Out of state?"

"I . . . I don't actually know. Mr. Barlowe has plans, I think." But if he did, he seemed strangely unwilling to share them with her.

"Tomorrow's the auction," she said on Friday. "Are you going to stay and watch as they sell off your family's things?"

He shook his head vehemently. "Dear God, no. I have no intention of witnessing that kind of farce."

But if Ellis had alternate plans for the day, he did not tell her. In the morning he made a quick trip into town with her truck and returned with a number of purchases: a new ladder of shiny aluminum, a new spade, rake and hoe, new hoses and a watering can. She was mystified. "Why would you buy this stuff, when—"

"It's for the next owner of this house. To help them keep up the gardens. I do hate to think of leaving them . . . untended."

She felt oddly moved by his gesture, and puzzled by it at the same time. Why hadn't he bought anything for the trip they were about to make? She wondered if he'd found another house on Wainscott Island, or maybe nearby, on the mainland.

Edna was back that afternoon, and Ellis spent most of the day in the barn with her, tagging along behind her as she lurched about excitedly, her cane stabbing at the floor, looking over the merchandise one more time, revising her list. Ellis seemed in an oddly benign, even amused, frame of mind; he regarded Edna with what seemed to be a pleasant, indulgent, even gracious sort of air, as if she were some sweet grandparent who needed to be humored. Edna, on the other hand, was nearly beside herself with anxiety and excitement. A museum official was actually coming up from Boston to examine a tiger-maple highboy, some embroidered bed hangings and other furnishings.

Rose took this time to pack her own belongings, all the clothes and things she'd brought from Connecticut, her pads and pencils. Ellis had not packed a single thing: His clothes, what few he actually had, were still sitting in a bureau that would be auctioned off in the morning. She took them out now and mixed them in with her own; then she went downstairs to organize her collection of teas and herbs. Certainly they would need these, wherever they went.

Ellis was silent, somber, when he came to bed that night, but he began his deliberate, lazy sort of foreplay on her. Gently stroking her arms and belly, then her thighs, his fingertips barely touching her skin. She lay still, letting him coax her slowly into arousal; then she gave way joyfully, opening her mouth and her legs to him. And it was, at first, wonderful, as passionate and effortless as in the beginning of the summer. They both laughed, as if in surprise at this, rolling about in the bed that would not be theirs the following day. She came quickly once, and then again, but he continued to thrash away . . .

No, she thought: Oh, no. She could see, even in the dark, the pained, anguished look on his face, as he struggled for his own orgasm, which seemed inexplicably out of his reach. He thrust harder and deeper, as if it were buried away deep inside her. Eventually he gave up, rolling away. He got up out of bed, and she heard him dressing, then pacing, out on the porch.

She lay awake, still achy from her own pleasure. And suddenly the pieces came together in her mind: his odd moods. His inability to climax. His calmness about selling the house but his refusal to tell her where they were going. *They* weren't going anywhere. Ellis was going to leave without her.

She leaped from the bed, pulling a sheet around her naked body, and ran out to the porch. Startled, he turned and looked at her in astonishment. "Rose—?"

"Ellis, you can't leave without me."

He frowned, as if not quite understanding her.

"Were you planning to do that?" Her voice dropped, as she pulled the sheet tighter around herself. "Are you going to go back to the priesthood?"

"Why would you think that?" He was astonished. "How can you think that?"

"Please don't leave me, Ellis. Let me come with you."

He came over to her and put his hands on her shoulders.

"Rose. Tell me the truth. How do you really, honestly feel about me?"

"Feel? Ellis, I *love* you."

At this his face seemed to soften a bit. "Then why couldn't you say it sooner?"

She felt a wave of guilt and sorrow. "Is that what this is all about, my not saying the words? Ellis, I'm sorry. They're hard words to say. I've never really said them to anyone before."

"So how do you expect me to know, if you don't say it?!" He shouted, suddenly angry. But then, just as abruptly, he embraced her, tightly. "I'm sorry. I'm sorry, Rose. I just so needed to *hear* it. Say it again."

"I love you."

"Yes, yes," he began kissing her, in a hungry, desperate way. "I love you, too. I'll never leave you. How could you think I would?" He kissed her again, soundly. "We'll be together forever, Rose," he whispered into her mouth. "Let's go, *now.*"

"Now?" She gazed up at the sky. It was night, the moon hidden by silvery clouds.

His eyes were actually glowing with some eerie inner light. "Yes! Now," he whispered, laughing as if it were the most wonderful idea in the world. And once again, she felt enchanted by those eyes, that boyish smile.

"Let me go and get dressed," she murmured.

"You don't have to . . ." she heard him say, and she hurried back into the house.

She emerged carrying her valise.

"I turned off all the lights. Should I leave a note for Edna and the real-estate lady?"

"No, no, don't bother." He grabbed her arm and pulled her over to her truck. "Come on, give me the keys."

"My truck? Oh, Ellis. It's not running well at all. Why can't we take your nice new car?"

"Give me the keys!" he snapped, with such anger she actually jumped. Puzzled, she placed them in his hand. He'd turned cold and tense on her and jerkily worked the truck out onto the road, speeding toward the wooden bridge to the mainland.

He rumbled across it at a frightening speed, then sped up the curving hill on the other side. Then, abruptly, he stopped the truck and made a K-turn in the middle of the road. His foot was on the brake; the truck was idling noisily.

"Did you change your mind?" she asked. He shook his head no. She turned and took a good look at him. He seemed, in the hazy moonlight, deathly pale, even trembling. He turned to her, his face filled with an unearthly, inexplicable fear.

"Rose," he began solemnly, "*do* you want to be with me, forever? For eternity?"

She stared at him without answering.

"This is the only way we can do it." He looked out the windshield at the island on the other side of the bridge, his eyes glittering. "I thought about concocting some sort of tea, or poison, for us to drink. But I couldn't bear the thought of anyone finding us. This is the best way, the quickest. Don't be afraid. It'll be a few minutes, a few bad minutes, but . . . don't fight it. Don't struggle, just let it happen." He stroked her leg in an anxious way, smiling weakly. "And then we'll be together. Eternally. In whatever circle of heaven."

"No," she whispered. "No, Ellis—"

"You should unhook your seat belt," he said, in a soft, tender way, moving to do so, but she slapped his hands away. "NO!" She screamed, pushing him. "Ellis, get out! Get out of this truck, now!"

He stared at her, as if betrayed. "You wanted this, you wanted to come with me—"

"Not like this, not like—ELLIS!"

In some mad act of anger, or defiance, he jammed his foot down onto the accelerator. Her old truck careened down the hill, and she began kicking at him, struggling to get at the brake pedal, unmindful of the seat belt that held her in place. After a few horrible moments, she felt the brake sink under her foot; the truck swerved and screeched to a crazy, sudden, thudding stop.

In an instant she saw Ellis fly up against the windshield, and then back again, his head slumping onto her shoulder. She turned off the ignition, and felt something wet soaking into her shirt. Then she saw the bloody splotch on the shattered windshield, where Ellis had hit. And she began screaming.

Headlamps shone across the bridge, and people were running across, thumping hard. And she continued to scream and scream, unable to stop. "I killed him!" she sobbed. "He's dead, and I killed him."

23

ROSE now made her way to the parlor of the Wainscott Point Inn, where she saw a man she had indeed not seen in many, many years.

Her brother-in-law, Graham Keating, stood in the middle of the room: Now a wizened, spindly sort of old man who employed a metal walker, he nevertheless glared up at her with a vigorous, youthful hatred. Her marriage to Burt, thirty years before, had caused an irreparable breach between the brothers. Burt, in his eagerness to help reestablish Rose's Connecticut nursery, had insisted the Keating Nursery he owned with Graham be put up for sale, and Graham was sure he'd been cheated somehow along the line. For many years they did not speak to each other, but had reached a grudging sort of truce about five years earlier, when Rose's now-adult children expressed an interest in their father's brother. Amanda and Hank had actually come up to visit him; and sometimes Graham called them, on holidays, though he never asked to speak to either Rose or Burt.

Now here he was, seeming old beyond belief, but Rose still recognized his foxlike triangular face, the blazing blue eyes so much like Burt's. He snickered.

"Yeah, it's you. I should've known. Thought I saw you cowering there in the back, in the church."

"You've become a Catholic?" she asked blandly, determined not to let him get to her. He snickered again.

"Oh, no, no. I went for the show. To see the masterful Father Barlowe give his talk. And how astounding, to see my sister-in-law there, running after the lover who dumped her. With a husband literally on his deathbed. Oh yes, I talked to your kids. Your daughter's quite worried about you. About your sanity."

Rose was stung by this, stung by the fact Amanda would confide in her uncle about her. But she did not react to Graham's taunt. "Burt knows I'm here."

"How can he, if he's a vegetable?"

"You don't know that. You haven't even spoken to the man, your own brother, in years. You haven't seen him in thirty."

"And whose fault is that? You've done nothing but take men away from me. Grubby, grasping Jew-woman. First Barlowe, and when you were done with him, my brother. And my business, my livelihood, along with him. I should've known you'd turn up. Once a tramp, always a tramp. You got wind Barlowe was back, so you're here to lure him away, to keep you company when Burt kicks off." He picked up his walker, pushing it forward in a menacing way. Rose said nothing: She actually felt sorry for him; he was so pathetically angry, the way her boys used to be when they were tots, wanting to wound, to hurt, and seemingly for no reason.

"Well, it's not going to work, Rosie. Because Barlowe, let me tell you, he's changed. A changed man. He's a fucking *saint* now, he won't have anything to do with the likes of you."

Tell me something I don't know, thought Rose. She sighed in an impatient way. "All right, you've vented your anger at me, old man," she said quietly. "Feel better? Why don't you go call my kids now, tell them I've gone off the deep end." She turned, but suddenly felt the metal legs of his walker up against her.

"Don't you want to know," Graham teased, in a wheedling, sly voice, "where he is?"

Rose paused without turning. "No."

"Bullshit. Of course you do, that's the whole reason you came running up here."

"You don't know where he is," Rose sputtered. "How would you, of all people, know?"

"I do know. You forget, Ellis was my friend   "

"Yes, before you grabbed his crotch and made him hit you."

"I want to take you to see him," Graham continued, unfazed. "I want to set up an audience for you, for the sheer pleasure of watching him humiliate you totally. I want to watch him set his bland cool eyes on you and say, 'The Lord be with you, my sister in Christ. Repent, repent . . .' " He cackled.

She turned to him. "Just tell me where he is."

"Oh, I can't do it, Rosie. Can't tell you." He grinned. "I have to show you. You have to come with me."

She stared at him. She knew Graham could be playing an elaborately cruel trick on her to repay her for whatever bad luck he felt she'd thrust upon him. Still, if there was one last chance she might see Ellis . . .

"All right," she snapped. "Then take me to him. Now."

He took her in his own ancient, rusting car back to what used to be the Keating Nursery. The fields were now dotted with half-built condominiums and cottages, but there was still one empty stretch of land that headed toward the sea. She waited patiently for Graham to maneuver himself and his walker out of the car and was startled when he began chugging along into the muddy, weedy field.

"Come on, come on, I don't have all day." He was already sweating, red-faced.

"What kind of trick is this?"

"It's no trick. This is still my land. My land."

They made their way over the ruts and small ditches.

"A piece of crap, this land," Graham was muttering. "Can't do nothing with it. Floods every spring. Developers don't want it. No more farmers around. That's what I get stuck with. Burt got the better of the deal—"

"Where are we going, Graham?" She was mystified. Perhaps she was following a madman.

He stopped and pointed.

"Oh," she said, softly. At the end of the field, facing the sea, well disguised now by some bushy shrubs, was the small stone outbuilding she'd noticed years and years ago, as she sat in the empty parking lot of Keating's Nursery, waiting out Ellis's wrath.

"He's . . . there?"

"Yeah, the old meetinghouse. I'd forgotten all about it. He remembered it. Said he needed a 'safe' place on this island, a 'hermitage,' he called it. Sort of a monastery away from home. It's full of mice and crap, but he didn't care. He said he just needed a place to think and pray." He gave Rose a withering smile. "I think he's gone round the bend, Rosie, finally. He always had that tendency, you know." He hurried ahead of her, racing toward the structure, his walker thumping into the dirt, then paused dramatically, waiting for her to catch up.

But Rose didn't move, paralyzed for the moment with fear of yet another blank rejection by Ellis; she couldn't bear those gray eyes, full of emptiness, focused on her again.

"Come on, woman! What are you waiting for, an invitation?"

Had she come all this way only to turn cowardly, to run away? She knew she would have to continue on and confront Ellis, no matter how painful or inadequate his reception of her would be.

Graham banged his walker against the old batten door with its iron strap hinges and rotting wood, which was already partially open. He banged once more. But there was no answer. Graham peered in.

"Gone," he muttered in grim surprise.

Rose exploded. "You were lying to me all along! This was all a trick, just to humiliate me!"

"I swear, it wasn't, Rose." He toddled over to a small table inside and showed Rose a note that had been left under a sea-smoothed rock. Instantly, she recognized Ellis's distinctive scrawl—

Graham: Many thanks for the use of the old cabin. I know you thought me odd for requesting it, but it did provide a tiny haven of necessary peace and solitude during my brief stay here, and helped enormously in helping me try to get my life, and soul, back in order. But now I have other tasks to attend to. I will remember you in my prayers upon my return to Benedetto. Please do consider the advice I gave you about reconciling with your brother. As you know, I myself have no great love or regard for Burt, but your last years should not be weighed down with such hatred and bitterness. Ellis.

Still clutching the note, Rose stumbled back out into the sun and looked about, wildly. Gone, she thought. She had come so close, only to miss him entirely. Why hadn't she at least spoken to him on the steps of the church? Why had she run away? She moaned and shook her head, swallowing back a huge lump of remorse and frustration, angry with herself.

Graham, seeming chastened, limped toward her. "Well, come on, old girl. I'll drive you back . . ."

She dropped the note and hurried away from him, walking down to the surf, making her way north along the beach back toward the inn. It was hard work, walking the stony, rocky shore, negotiating fat granite boulders slick with algae and crusted with barnacles. But she continued on grimly, castigating herself with every step. Her children, she thought, were right: She'd gone crazy, loony in her old age, running after a phantom lover from the past. Leaving her good, faithful husband behind, hovering between life and death. If there is a God, she thought, surely He is punishing me now for being so foolish and ungrateful, so very unwise.

The mile or so to the Wainscott Point Inn seemed endless, as rocks bit into her sneakered soles, the sun burned her eyes and brine and fish rot assaulted her nose. She shielded her face and looked up, toward the Inn, as it finally came into sight. She saw people moving about, guests departing, and a man standing on the porch, a tall man whose stance was so similar to Ellis's that she had to look away. When she looked again, the man was crossing the lawn, coming in her direction, toward the cliff that led down to the sea: a man in casual clothes, white shirt and khaki pants, snowy white hair blowing in the wind.

No, she thought: My mind is playing tricks. I'm wishing for it, too much, to be Ellis.

But it was Ellis, standing at the top of the cliff, now crouching down, offering his hand to help her up. Smiling, with what clearly seemed to be both recognition . . . and joy.

24

Rose was struggling to awaken from a leaden sleep. She felt a hand, someone's hand, grazing her face—

"Ellis," she murmured. She opened her eyes and saw Burt Keating's lumpy features, his coppery hair.

"Hey, Rose. You're coming 'round."

Her eyes traveled past him, looking about the room. A stark, mint-green room that reminded her of a—

"Hospital," she whispered. "Oh, my God." The sudden remembrance of what had happened filled her with a dark, inky sickness. Her hand went to her shoulder, and she felt the stiffness of dried blood on her shirt. "Ellis is dead," she whispered.

"No, no, Rose. He's okay."

"Okay?" She didn't understand this.

"Well, that was quite a bump he took on his head. They got him stitched up downstairs, but they'll probably keep him a few days, until his brain clears up."

"His brain?"

"The police were trying to talk to him about the accident. But apparently he wasn't making much sense."

"I have to see him." She began to get up, but felt her head swim in a violent way. "Oh, what's wrong, what's wrong with me?"

"You had to be sedated for a while. You were raving, not making much sense yourself. Shock, the doctors called it."

"I have to see Ellis."

But Burt firmly, though pleasantly, placed his hands on her shoulders. "You're not going anywhere. Yet." She struggled feebly against him as a cheery nurse strolled in.

"Oh, good, she's awake. We can check her out as soon as we make sure she's okay." She glanced at Burt. "You the boyfriend, or whatever?"

"Yep," he said quickly. "I'll take care of her."

"I have to see Ellis," she whimpered.

"You've had a shock," said the nurse, "so we gave you a little something to calm you down. But you have no injuries, and luckily nothing happened to the baby."

Rose stared at her. "What baby?"

The nurse now looked uncomfortable. "Well, of course you were examined in the emergency room. Our resident obstetrician guessed you were seven or eight weeks into your first trimester. Didn't you, uh, know?"

"It's impossible. A mistake," she whispered.

"Now take it easy. Of course, you should go and get the blood test done."

"I have to see Ellis. Please." She grabbed Burt by the arm. "Take me to him, please. I need to see him."

He looked mournful, his mouth downcast in a sad, disapproving way.

"Okay. I'll take you down."

She found Ellis lying in bed, encased in a cervical collar, his forehead taped up, his face nearly buried. His eyes were shut so tightly she could not tell if he was asleep or merely in pain. But when she touched him, he didn't stir.

"Ellis," she said, softly, into his ear. He groaned, as if struggling on some level to respond to her. She touched his face again, dismayed at how waxy and cool it felt. "I'm sorry," she crooned. "I had to do it. I had to stop you . . ." She looked up and saw a doctor on the other side of the bed, frowning at her.

"Father Barlowe should be fine. He's suffered a serious concussion and needs to be observed for the next few days or so, but there's no reason to be—"

"You said . . . Father Barlowe . . . ?"

"He did manage to tell us who he was."

"He called himself Father?"

"Yes. . . . He told us he was the assistant pastor of St. Cyril's parish, in Wisterville, Connecticut."

"He's not a priest anymore! He left!"

The doctor now regarded her in a worried way.

"The pastor of that parish did not tell us that. He said that Father Barlowe was on vacation, and that he himself was coming right up to take care of things—"

"No, no, you can't let him take him, you can't let him take Ellis—"

"Rose." Burt was now pulling her, gently, from Ellis's bedside. "No one can take Barlowe anywhere right now."

"Leave me alone!"

"Let me take you . . . home with me."

"I don't want to go home with you."

"Rose, you need your rest. Barlowe needs his rest. Come on." He put his big arms about her and literally dragged her out into the hall.

"I'm not going anywhere with you," she cried. "Take me back to my home, at Ellis's."

"You don't want to go there."

"Yes, I do. Take me there."

He shrugged and helped her check out of the hospital. ("The police," one of the nurses said ominously, "still want to talk to you.") They drove back onto the island in the dark, in silence, Rose shutting her eyes tightly as they drove over the wooden bridge, the rumble of it almost physically painful for her. They finally reached the old Barlowe manse, just a dark silhouette against the night sky.

"The auction was today," said Burt in a flat voice. "I guess it went over big. Nothing left, I hear." He turned to Rose. "You'd be more comfortable with me and Graham."

"No."

"I won't let you stay here alone."

"Burt, please."

"How about if I stay in my truck?"

It was as if she heard, for the first time, the concern and caring in his voice. She felt a rush of guilt and remorse.

"You needn't do that. You've been too good to me already. I don't deserve it."

"You don't deserve this, Rose." When she didn't answer, he continued, "I'll be back, then, in the morning. Bring you breakfast."

She nodded, weakly grateful.

"Rose? Where was you and Barlowe going?"

"Nowhere."

"But how—"

"He was driving too fast. And he stopped too fast. That's all there is to it." She sighed and stepped out of the truck. "Good night, Burt."

She walked up the stairs into the empty house. Inexplicably, her valise sat in front of the door, the valise she'd packed to take with her, when she and Ellis finally fled. Had she merely forgotten it, or had some kind soul fished it out of her truck? She felt some gratefulness for it none-theless, for it contained all her worldly goods, her precious sketches.

She picked it up and hugged it as she wandered through the empty, now cavernous house. It was littered with paper and debris now, the floors scuffed, the kitchen table filled with coffee cups and empty bakery boxes. In the back, the striped tent still stood, flaps rippling in the breeze off the sea. She went to the bedroom, and to her surprise found it still furnished: Obviously the bed had been overlooked in the heat of the auction. She sank into it gratefully, drawing the linens and sheets close around her.

It still smelled of him, of them, of the sex they had to-gether in it. Only one day had passed, and yet their lives had changed profoundly. She knew already: He was gone now, lost to her forever. How could she return to a man who'd tried to kill her?

How? How? And yet it seemed to her she had no other choice, such was the intensity of her love for him. He had not, she reasoned with herself, tried to kill her out of hatred or malice, but only because he did indeed love her so much in return; he only wanted to be with her, in some pain-free paradise, forever. He did not want to die alone. She knew little about psychology or psychotherapy, but she did un-derstand Ellis was suffering from some sickness of the mind and spirit. If she could take him away, far away somewhere, perhaps she could help . . .

But there was another life now. The baby, she knew, that she had to keep. It was unexpected, a miracle, a true gift. And it was Ellis, coming to life inside her. There was no question in her mind that she would keep it, though already she dreaded the actual prospect of it, another crushing prac-tical responsibility, when she already had to deal somehow with Ellis.

It'll work out, somehow, she thought, growing sleepy again. An odd little family. Together, for eternity . . .

She awoke, still dressed, feeling hot, sticky and slightly nauseous, to the sound of banging on the front door. There stood Burt Keating, with a bright grin, an absurdly hopeful expression on his face. He handed her a paper sack.

"Something for you to eat."

"I'm not at all hungry."

"When was the last time you ate?"

"I don't know. I don't care."

"Well, that's fine for you, Rose Connolly. But what about that baby you're carrying?"

She glanced into the bag, sullenly. There were several pieces of fruit, bananas, apples, and several muffins he must have picked up at the bakery on the mainland. She picked up one of these and bit into it: It was still warm, an odd sort of comfort.

"Brought you some coffee, too."

"Oh, I don't drink that stuff. . . . Well, let me have a sip." It was bitter, but surprisingly bracing; she went for another gulp.

"The police been by yet?"

She stared at him in horror.

"What business is it of theirs?" she snapped.

"They seem to think, for some reason, that"—he looked extremely uneasy, his deep blue eyes darting away—"you and Barlowe were aiming to drive off the bridge. You know, a crazy suicide sort of thing. I know that can't be true, can it, Rose? Not even Barlowe is that crazy—"

Rose burst into tears, clapping her hands over her face, shuddering with great, heaving sobs. Burt said nothing. He merely sat and watched as she wept. And when she began to slow down, he said, softly, "So. That's how it was."

She jumped up. "I should prepare some tea for him. Some of his headache tea. I'm sure he'll need it now—" She actually chuckled in a grim way. "What can I put it in? A thermos? I think it's been auctioned off—" She tried to chuckle again, but another sob came out. Burt clamped his hand over hers.

"Never mind the tea. That's not going to help him now."

"I have to see him," she whispered.

His shoulders sagged in a defeated way. "I hope you're planning on changing your clothes."

She looked down at her brown, blood-splattered chambray shirt. Feeling the stain with her fingers, it felt stiff, old, a nightmare of the past, like the stains on Doctor Barlowe's bed.

Once she was at the hospital, she stopped just short of Ellis's room, sensing some commotion, something going on in the room: a gathering of some sort, quiet, serious talking. She turned to Burt, who'd been clumping along behind her; he seemed to have guessed her thoughts.

"Okay, Rose, I'll wait out here. I'll just go down the hall a bit."

She peered in the doorway. She saw Ellis still supine, his head in wraps, motionless, and by his bedside, three priests. Too late she recognized the monsignor from St. Cyril's: She tried to dart away, but his voice boomed out the door.

"Mrs. Connolly!"

She stopped in her tracks. Caught, guilty, she turned and faced the stocky, bald man who'd once been her pastor, even a remote, polite friend. The monsignor regarded her in a serious way, without anger or even curiosity.

"So," he said, with a small smile. "The rumors were true. About you running away with our Father Ellis."

She nodded, stiffening, preparing herself for the condemnation, the lecture she was sure would follow—the inevitable blast of icy anger, the stern paternalistic rebuke.

"Seems so odd. So odd. You're a lovely girl, Rose. But you don't seem Barlowe's type at all."

She shrugged, puzzled at his warmth and casualness.

"I mean, I never thought he was much interested in women at all. If you know what I mean." Now he shrugged in a sheepish, apologetic way. "I guess I have no real intuition, about these things. Unless . . . it was some kind of platonic—"

"No. No. We were lovers." She looked him in the eye, then without knowing why, added, "We were going to be married. Somehow."

"Ah," the monsignor said, softly. "I don't suppose you'll be wanting to marry him now. After what's happened. After what you've been through with him."

She stared at him.

"He told us something about it all, in a very disjointed way. I understand now how deeply troubled he was. I had no idea. It's very serious, Rose. Very serious. When any man tries to take his own life, and the life of another. But when it's a fellow priest . . ." He shook his head in a helpless, sorrowful way, and Rose could see it was almost beyond his comprehension. Her eyes burned with tears.

"I still think . . . I can help him, Father—"

"We're making arrangements," he said, as if not hearing her, "to transport him to a special hospital in Pennsylvania. It's at a monastery that specializes in the care of troubled priests. Troubled men—"

"No," she whispered. "Oh, no."

"Rose, he's no use to you now. He's of no use to anyone now. He needs help." He took her by the elbows. "And he may decide eventually to come back to you, and be your husband, but right now we have an obligation to help him. For many years he served us as a good, loyal, conscientious priest, and now it's our turn to help him. He has to be healed mentally, and spiritually, and emotionally, before he can make any kind of rational decision about his future."

She merely bowed her head.

"Rose? Is there anything we can do for you?"

"Just let me see him one more time. Alone."

She stood over his bed and cupped his face in her hands. "Ellis."

He gazed up at her in an odd, suspicious, almost fearful way.

"You have to get better. You have to! You have to come back to me. You said it was for eternity. Forever."

He continued to stare at her. His eyes, slightly bloodshot, seemed foggy, blank.

"I'll be waiting. I'll wait for you, here," she whispered urgently into his face. But nothing seemed to be registering. His eyes were indeed blank, uncomprehending. And she realized, with a chill, that he was no longer her Ellis, but had passed into another phase of his life, one that surely would no longer include her.

And yet she waited for him. She spent the longest month of her life in Ellis's empty house, watching summer days shorten and grow cool. The trees on the mainland began to change color, and school buses rumbled over the wooden bridge to collect the island's children. She tended the garden, pulling out the spent and wasted plants, trimming back the perennials in preparation for winter, drying what remained of the tea herbs. And her belly began to expand slightly, her breasts growing larger: She didn't need a blood test to tell her what she already knew.

Burt kept his distance, but left gifts on the porch steps: food, baskets of apples and winter squash, firewood, even thick sweaters and flannel shirts. Sometimes she ran out to thank him, but he would be gone before she made it to the porch.

And finally, as September was coming to an end, she had a letter from Ellis: Her heart pounded when she saw the Pennsylvania postmark and his thin, spidery scrawl across the envelope. But the envelope was heartbreakingly thin, the letter little more than a paragraph. She sat down on the front steps to read it:

Dearest Rose:

You must no longer wait for me, but go home to your little farm and house in Connecticut and resume your life. I cannot allow you to suffer with me any longer. My head is healed, but I am still so confused and sick about my life; I don't believe I shall ever be truly whole again. Benedetto is a calm and peaceful sort of place, however, and perhaps the best chance I have of getting well is to remain here. You may stay at my house a little longer, but I'm arranging with my lawyer for its sale. I wish only the best for you, Rose, and I'm sorry for everything I've put you through these past few months.

She stared at the letter, at the graceful, almost delicate handwriting, stung by the briefness, the coolness of it. There was no mention of "forever" or "eternity" in it, or even love for that matter: He had simply signed it, "Ellis." Years later she would reread it and would see in the tight, polite phrases the shame and remorse he felt, his agony and confusion. But now her hands trembled as she held it, her whole body aquiver with hurt, sorrow and dismay.

And this is where Burt Keating found her, later that afternoon: still sitting on the top step of the porch, clutching the letter, shivering in the chilly autumn air, but incapable of moving.

"What can I do, Rose?" he asked desperately, hugging her in a clumsy way, rubbing her arms with his big, dusty hands.

"Take me back," she whispered. "Take me away from here. Back to Connecticut."

25

LUCAS worked feverishly alongside Rose's son Tommy, out in the nursery's distant fields, chopping down some brambles that had overtaken Keating territory. He was trying to stay as far from Amanda as he could, mortified by their encounter in bed that morning, and feeling, at the same time, utterly trapped. He had no money, no car, no way of escaping, and he felt a moral, gentlemanly obligation to wait for Rose, or word from her, before embarking on his own life. But his thoughts about Theo were achingly, painfully clear: He had become obsessed in an unhealthy way with the older monk, and there was nothing mystical or lofty about it. It was all sexual, physical, rooted firmly in his groin. And then there was Amanda, attractive only because of her resemblance to her father. Not that the idea of an encounter with her as a woman so repelled him: He'd felt that uneasy erotic pull toward her, that curiosity, from the start, though he was still convinced his real desire was for other men. But he was infuriated at her for using him, as if he were some kind of dumb, erect animal, a sort of masturbatory device. The world, he thought, is full of such people, self-centered, greedy for their own pleasure. Was he so certain he wanted to plunge back into it?

Tommy grabbed his arm suddenly and pointed in a stern way to a clump of shiny greenery. Lucas nodded: poison ivy, a plant he'd always been immune to. He whacked at it nonchalantly, as Tommy thunked, thunked, thunked away at the brambles with his axe. Thunk, thunk, and suddenly Lucas heard an odd muted sound, as if the ax had hit some soft piece of fruit.

Tommy came loping toward him, grinning. His jeans' leg was torn and red with blood. Lucas yelped.

"Guess I need a Band-Aid, Luke. Look, it won't stop bleeding."

Lucas leaped over toward him and ripped away the leg of his jeans. He saw a fairly serious gaping wound, bleeding copiously. He tore off the T-shirt he was wearing and ripped it into a makeshift bandage and tourniquet. Then spotted, in the grass, the green spikes and fat round leaves of the weed plantain. Hadn't Theo told him it was a wound herb with styptic, healing properties? He wasn't sure, but plucked a few of the big leaves nonetheless, then carefully laid them over the wound, underneath the bandage of T-shirt material. He then struggled to pull Tommy—who was a full head taller than he and certainly heavier—across the fields.

"But I'm okay. You fixed it."

"You need stitches. Come on! Amanda!" he shouted frantically. "Hank! Somebody, help!"

Amanda came hurrying out of the retail store, stopping short when she saw her brother. "Oh, Thomas," she muttered. "It's always something with you. And of course it has to be when Mom is—"

"Shut up!" Lucas snapped. "He has to go to the hospital, now. He needs to have his leg sewn up."

"All right, all right." Amanda locked up the shop, jangling her keys in an irritated way. Lucas snatched them from her.

"I'll take him."

Amanda eyed him with grim amusement. "Think the hospital will let you in without a shirt?"

Startled, Lucas glanced down at his bare chest, then hurtled into the house for his brown sweater. "Don't leave without me!" he shouted. He retrieved the sweater, then paused, taking along another T-shirt Amanda had given him, and his wallet, which, of course, was empty. Everything he owned in the world. He'd made, in that split second, a decision.

Somewhat to his surprise, Amanda had waited: Her truck was idling noisily; her arm was slung out the window, fingers tapping impatiently on the door. But as he approached, she opened the driver's side door, and scooted aside to let him behind the wheel. Tommy, scrunched against the passenger door, studied his reddening bandages with mild concern.

At the emergency room, they ran into the affable cardiologist Dr. Tan, who seemed delighted to see them. "Hello Keatings!" he crowed, then gave Tommy's leg an admiring glance. "Hey, nice job! How'd you do that?"

"With an ax," said Tommy, with some pride.

Dr. Tan lingered on as another doctor, an older man with a sour face, poked at Tommy's bandages with latex-gloved hands. The older doctor grimaced in disgust and picked off the now-sodden plantain leaves with tweezers.

But Dr. Tan was intrigued. "Hey, man, what's that stuff?"

"Plantain," Lucas murmured. "Used in ancient times to stanch battle wounds."

"Cool! I'm taking a seminar on homeopathic medicines. Herbs and that kind of stuff. Are you some kind of healer-guy?"

"He's a monk," Amanda offered playfully, and Dr. Tan bobbed his head in approval.

"Oh yeah, spiritual healing, combined with technology and traditional methods— It's the wave of the future, man! This is the medicine of the twenty-first century, no kidding!"

Lucas, feeling oddly flattered, wandered out into the hall-way, while Tommy was being stitched up. He felt vaguely at home here, in this small-town hospital, even though it was far busier and less peaceful than Benedetto's infirmary. Instead of gray-robed monks silently sweeping in and out of rooms, nurses—both male and female—clad in white or aqua or peach whisked about, chatting or laughing or talk-ing seriously. He watched them for a while, then turned, sensing Amanda beside him.

"Luke, I'm sorry." She actually sounded contrite. He studied her face. He'd never heard Theo apologize for any-thing, but if he ever had to, Lucas imagined he'd probably look the way his daughter did now, her gray eyes baleful, the corners of her mouth turned down in sullen annoyance.

"No, I'm sorry, Amanda."

"Don't be stupid! What do you have to be sorry for?"

"I called you Theo. I can't believe I did that, but . . . it really woke me up. It made me realize I have to get over him."

"You guys weren't really involved with each other, were you?"

"No. Theo was barely aware of my existence. And if your mom were to find him and bring him back, he would be completely baffled, I'm sure, by my desperate interest in him. He would be irritated, but worst of all, he'd probably feel . . . pity for me. This is as far as my connection with Theo goes." He then laughed. "Sleeping with his daughter. That's far enough, I'd say."

"I just want you to know, I don't have any diseases, or anything. And I'm on the pill. I don't want you to worry, because I have the feeling you're a worrier."

He nodded.

"I am sorry, Lucas." Her face softened. "Your first time, it should be special. Though mine wasn't . . . But it should be. I sort of robbed you of that."

"It's okay, Amanda. I intend to go out and have another 'first time' eventually."

She nodded, puzzled. He placed his hand on his chest.

"I have everything I own on me. This sweater, this T-shirt you gave me, these jeans." He glanced down. "Splattered with your brother's blood. All my earthly possessions. I'm not going back to the farm with you and Tommy. I want you to drop me off at the nearest bus station. I'm going to take the next bus into Hartford."

"You have money?"

"Well, no—"

"Then we'll stop at an ATM machine. But are you sure you don't want to wait for Mom to get back?"

He shook his head solemnly. "I can't wait around anymore. I have to make a start, sometime."

"You're not going back to the monastery?"

"No. I'm tempted to . . . It would be the easiest thing to do, though I'd be doing penance until eternity. But I don't feel I belong there anymore." He paused. "I have a sister in Hartford. Stacy. She's a social worker. Of all my brothers and sisters, she's the one I always liked best. I haven't spoken with her in years, but I think she'll put me up."

Amanda looked relieved. "Well, Hartford's not so far away. You can come back for a visit. Pick your own produce. I'm sure you'll want to talk to Mom again, at some point in the future. When you're settled, when you've had a chance to achieve some distance."

"And what are you going to do, Amanda?"

She set a hand on her hip. "About what?" she asked, tersely.

"You know. The rest of your life."

"Oh, that." She shrugged. "I just don't have the luxury of thinking about that now. Maybe when Mom returns, and my father dies . . ." Her voice dropped to a whisper. "That could be very, very soon, I suppose."

Tommy came limping out, still cheerful. He displayed his properly bandaged limb with great pleasure.

"Wonderful, Tommy," Amanda crooned. "Mom will be delighted to see it, I'm sure." She then hooked her arm around his and Lucas's.

"Come on. Before we take you to the bus, let's go upstairs to ICU, and I'll introduce you to my real father."

26

Rose and Ellis now walked together, through the Victorian gardens of the Wainscott Point Inn in the waning hours of the afternoon, as high tide swept over the rocky shore below.

"I'm just grateful you hadn't checked out yet," Ellis was saying. "I'd been thinking of you, but never expected to encounter you up here. But why did you run away from me like that after Mass?"

"I thought you didn't recognize me." She felt giddy, schoolgirlish, her heart pounding.

"You didn't give me a chance to. Before I could even blink, you were gone. I actually thought I'd only imagined that it was you. You've been on my mind the whole time I've been here; I thought somehow I'd conjured you up. But when I called the Wainscott Inn—I knew if you came back, this is where you'd be—they told me that you were, indeed, a guest here. I couldn't believe it."

"But why did you come here, of all places, Ellis? And if

you wanted to see me, why didn't you just come to Connecticut?"

"It's complicated, Rose. I know you're wrapped up with
Burt, and your children; I didn't want to disturb you at this
time. I know you have a difficult decision to make about
him. And I've been busy, preoccupied, myself. I've been on
a long journey elsewhere, and I had no intentions of even
coming up here. This hasn't exactly been a vacation, Rose:
I've been engaged in a task, in duty, something to do with
my life and work as a priest, a member of the Benedetto
community. Coming here was a spur-of-the-moment decision: I was at the end of my trip, I had a little time and the
opportunity, and I thought it couldn't hurt to confront some
old ghosts. One last time," he murmured, adding a grim
chuckle.

"You never mentioned in your letters that you were going away. And your abbot was so mysterious about it."

"You spoke with Dom Gervase? On the phone?"

"No, face-to-face. I went to Benedetto."

"You were . . . there?" He seemed both awed and amused.

"Yes, I went there, because you stopped writing to me.
Ellis, I was so worried about you."

He turned from her.

"I wasn't able to write about it. I've been going through
a difficult time, Rose."

"Were you thinking of leaving?"

He didn't answer, but instead took a seat on a bench
under a sprawling wisteria vine, stretching his long legs out
in front of him. "What was your impression of the abbey?"

"It seemed such a very odd place," she said, tentatively,
taking a seat beside him. "That unearthly quiet, and the
very remoteness of it, on that mountaintop. Nothing but
men. But it did seem a place of peace, of calm. I can understand why . . . you stayed there, remained there, all these
years."

He said nothing, his eyes focused on her face. They seemed blue again, matching the summer sky.

"How does it feel," she asked him, "to be here, again?"

He looked around. "It's startling, really, even a bit unsettling. Because this isn't the place it was, when we . . . It's no longer what it was, a haunted estate reeking of death and pain. I do give those innkeepers credit for transforming it, making it into a place of welcome, however bizarre." He chuckled. "They've redeemed it." His smile faded. "I believed once I would never set foot on this island again. I did actually feel some distress, driving across that bridge. But the memories really did not begin to come flooding back . . . until I saw you."

"Good memories," she ventured. "Or bad?"

He regarded her somberly for a long time. "Rose, I've never quite been able to broach this subject in our correspondence. Perhaps I've been afraid to, afraid of what I might hear. But now that I'm here with you, for the first time in so many years, I have to ask you . . . Why? Why did you desert me back then, abandon me when I needed you most?"

She was shocked, almost beyond words. "I . . . I *didn't*, Ellis."

"I waited for you," he murmured, color flooding his cheekbones. "I waited for days, months, all in vain. I felt imprisoned, trapped, at Benedetto, those first few weeks. I thought you might come for me, or at least write . . ." His voice dropped. "Was I so awful to you that you had to hurt me, wound me so badly? Was I that cruel?"

"Ellis!" She was profoundly shocked. "You wrote me that note!"

"What note?"

"Ordering me to go home and forget about you. Arranging with your lawyer for the sale of the house! How was I supposed to respond to that?"

He didn't answer. She could see by the pained, baffled expression on his face that he didn't remember it at all.

"If I sent you such a note," he began, slowly, "it was to test you, I suppose. Prompt you into responding. I needed word from you, Rose. I was desperate for it. That much I do remember."

She shook her head despairingly. "We're both remembering this in completely different ways. Either one of us is mistaken, or there's been a terrible misunderstanding."

"I remember well enough," he snapped. "That letter, from your husband—"

"Burt wrote you?"

"How did you think I learned of your marriage?"

She drew in a deep breath. "I asked the monsignor to tell you."

"Yes, he told me, too. But Keating beat him to it. He was positively gloating, and let me know you were 'safe' and that if I ever returned to Maine, he would have me prosecuted on some ludicrous trumped-up charge, assault or attempted murder! He's been a torment to me all my life: Bullying me when I was a boy, then coming after you while we were living together. He wanted you, went after you and won you. But the mystery to me is why you wanted him, of all people."

She didn't answer: She felt utterly dismayed by this revelation, which seemed completely out of character for her otherwise decent husband. Yet she remembered Burt's dark contempt for Ellis in the months following their marriage: how he'd muttered, endlessly, that Ellis should have been arrested, "made to pay" for what he'd done to Rose and their unborn child.

"It wasn't . . . it couldn't have been sexual. Oh, Rose. You couldn't have loved him. And you certainly didn't need his farm or business or money."

"He was . . . safe." She hugged herself. "There was a

strength, a steadiness in him I'd never known before in a man. I'm so sorry, Ellis, but I needed that. After you, after everything we'd been through. I never loved him as much as he loved me; and I never loved him with the passion I had for you. But I did grow to care for him in time, over the years, as a friend, a companion. That I can't change or deny."

"How is it," he asked in a wan, despairing way, "you were able to have children with him, and not with me?"

She froze. Yet another Pandora's box. She had no choice but to tell him; there might not be another time.

"I only had two babies with Burt. My boys."

He stared at her. "What are you telling me, Rose? You have a daughter, you have . . . a daughter. Amanda." He clapped his hands over his face. "Oh, my God. *Amanda.*"

"She does resemble you, a great deal," Rose said, softly.

For a long time, he did not speak, his face still hidden from her. She saw that he was actually shaking with emotion.

"How," he whispered. "How could you keep this from me? How dare you keep this . . . this truth, from me, this child. What is she, thirty years old now?"

"I thought . . . I truly believed I was helping you at the time, Ellis. I didn't think you needed the pressure of an unexpected child, that overwhelming sort of responsibility—"

"You were helping me?" he shouted. "By deserting me, abandoning me, then depriving me of my only child—"

"You were CRAZY!" Rose shrieked back. She then sank back on the bench, aghast at the word that had emerged from her lips. "Yes," she continued, wearily, "you were mentally *ill*, Ellis. I'm sorry, but that's the bleak, honest truth. You needed professional help, and if I didn't come running back to you at that time, maybe it was because I knew, on some level, I couldn't handle it anymore. You tried to *kill* me, for God's sake. You haven't forgotten that, have you?"

He paled, a look of horror crossing his face. She drew back from him.

"Oh, my God. You don't remember. You don't remember, about trying to run us into the sea, with the truck—"

"I can't," he whispered. "I can't have done that, Rose. I'd remember that . . ."

"Don't you remember us fighting over the steering wheel, my hitting the brake—somehow, miraculously—with my foot. And you, smacking right into the windshield. Don't you remember how you ended up at Benedetto, why they sent you there in the first place?"

He shook his head, swallowing hard. "I knew . . . I knew I'd been in some kind of accident. I'd suffered some head trauma. And my therapist at Benedetto kept telling me it was a suicide attempt and I accepted that, but . . . but . . ." He stared at her wildly, then suddenly bolted from the bench and stalked out to the edge of the cliff, over-looking the sea. She dashed out after him and found him standing there, tears flooding down his face.

"I didn't know," he whispered. "I didn't know you were with me, too. I had nightmares about it, you and I trapped in a car, in a truck, underwater, but I couldn't connect those dreams with any specific incident. And when the accident was described to me . . . They never mentioned you, they never said you were there, too. Fellow priests: They were probably embarrassed, ashamed for me. Oh, Rose. Oh, Rose!" He turned to her. "How could you forgive me, after such a thing?"

"I've never thought of it in terms of sin or forgiving. Burt called it a crime, but to me it was simply a tragic sort of mistake, something almost beyond our power to control. For years I even blamed myself for it, thinking if only I'd done something for you sooner—"

He took her arm. "All these years, I thought you'd simply

ceased to care about me, had abruptly stopped loving me—"

"I could never stop loving you, Ellis," she whispered. "Why else would I be here now?"

"The fact that you are," he said, with emotion, "is a miracle."

"Have you forgotten everything else?" she asked, softly. "About your father . . . ?"

"I do remember," he said, sobering suddenly, wiping his face. "Him. How he died. But there are huge gaps in my memory now. It feels like a computer screen that's slowly fading or dissolving into gibberish. I remember bits and pieces of events or conversations, but nothing adds up to a whole, complete picture." He turned to her, suddenly taking her by the shoulders in an unexpectedly tender way. "I re-member you, Rose. I remember the pleasure of our love-making, and our garden, and the quiet summer days we shared. It remains firmly in my mind as a kind of Eden I experienced once, a sort of oasis in the long desert of my life. What I didn't remember was the end of it, the end of us. I remember only that awful . . . accident, something I sensed was my fault without knowing why. That is, pre-cisely, why I came back here. To remember. To try to put all the pieces together. I really wish I could know, before I die, what my life was about."

Rose shivered, sensing the waning of the day, the coming of night.

"You're not . . . You're not dying, are you, Ellis?" She asked the question in a tiny, hesitant voice: To her utter dismay, he turned to her and actually smiled wanly.

"You're *not!*" she demanded, terrified now.

"Rose, I'm an old man! Do you think I'll live forever? No, I'm not dying, not this minute, anyway."

"Ellis, tell me the truth! Where have you been these past two months?"

He took a deep breath. "At a clinic, in Boston—"

She moaned, not wanting to hear more. But he took her hand, in a consoling way. "I've been *working* there, Rose. At an AIDS hospice for the indigent and urban poor. That's been the pretext for this entire trip. I brought some of my herbs and teas with me, but mainly I've been working as a counselor, a consoler, a confessor. It's been an unexpectedly productive trip, and I've learned a great deal from it. I've been enriched by it . . ."

"And yet, it was not the real reason you left Benedetto."

"That's true, I'm afraid. I needed to be away from the abbey for a while. And from the very beginning, I wanted only to come here. Back to Maine, back to this wretched island. Because I needed desperately to remember and to understand: my past, the sins, the mistakes, the missteps. So I can make peace with it all, be at peace, finally."

"Weren't you happy at Benedetto? I thought you were."

He sighed. "I've found some measure of comfort and contentment. But in all my years there I've never been able to shake the feeling of being unworthy, undeserving, soiled somehow in the eyes of God. For years I would wake up and think: *I failed in my vocation.* And for years I've been trying to atone for it, while at the same time shoving it all to the back of my brain, not thinking about it, trying to forget I ever had any kind of life before Benedetto. For a while, I was actually able to keep myself busy enough to not think of it. That's why I've always been so careful, so remote, in my letters to you. I even tried to reimagine you as a completely different woman than the one I slept with, made love to, and loved."

"I . . . I sensed that, Ellis. It hurt, but I kept hoping, in time, that would change . . ."

"It all began to catch up with me this year. My headaches grew worse, and I found myself sinking into a dangerous sort of depression: I began quarreling with the other monks, neglecting my patients, and I was edging closer to the kind of crisis of faith that drove me away, out of the Church once before. I finally came to the realization that I was only half a man, half a priest, half a monk: I could no longer deny or disown that whole first half of my life. I wanted to confront the evil in it, but also remember the goodness in it, too, the evidence of God's love and caring there.

"But I couldn't just leave Benedetto, you know. When I transferred into that community, I took a whole new set of vows, of obedience, of commitment to my brothers there. It was the abbot who suggested I combine the trip with a worthy gesture, spend six weeks or so at that inner-city clinic, then come here to look after my heart and soul. He is a most wise and generous man. For even before I left the clinic to come here, I'd already come to an important conclusion about my life at Benedetto."

"What was that?"

"That I cannot leave. That I must return to Benedetto and spend the rest of my days there—"

"Why? To keep trying to make up for everything, to atone—"

"No, Rose," he said, with a quiet certainty. "Because it's my home. It's as simple as that: It's my home, my place. It's where I belong now; it's where my spiritual battles have to be fought from now on. I must go back; and every day I'm away deprives the men who are in my care."

"I know. . . . These are indeed stolen moments, for both of us. I should be with Burt. I should be at his bedside, right now." At the mention of Burt's name, she saw him stiffen and turn away. She was astounded.

"Does it hurt you for me to speak of him?"

"His name still cuts through me like a knife. I know he was your husband for thirty years and treated you decently. But it's always made me shudder to think of you with him."

"Please, please don't talk like this, Ellis. You told Graham to reconcile with Burt."

"Well, I had to, didn't I? I must continue to preach forgiveness, even if I can't quite manage it myself."

She swallowed. "Hearing you speak of Burt like that feels like . . . a negation of my life, of everything I've been through the past thirty years. My life as a wife, a mother, a business partner. Oh, Ellis. I wish you and I had remained together; I wish I had been your wife. But it didn't happen, and out of all that tragedy, two perfectly decent lives arose: yours at Benedetto, mine with Burt and the children. You don't regret what our lives have evolved into, do you?"

"No, no, of course not, Rose." He took her hands. "I'm only astounded that you continue to care for a man like me, who caused you so much sorrow. And I am so very moved, and touched, that you would come to seek me out now, considering your own circumstances."

"Yes, well . . . my kids think I'm crazy, of course. But I had to come and make sure you were all right."

His grip on her hands tightened.

"Does Amanda know that I'm—"

She nodded, quickly.

"I suppose I should contact her, in some way. Talk with her. I'm a little afraid to, Rose. I don't know what I should say. I never imagined I would ever have a child."

"Oh, Ellis, I am so very sorry. I should never, ever, have kept that from you. That was unforgivable, on my part."

"Do you have a picture of her?"

"Of course. In my purse, I think." She led him back toward the house. He took her arm, and they strolled across the lawn to the mansion. They exchanged a smile of complicity at the delightful oddness of returning together to the house they alone once shared. They hurried through the overwrought decor of the parlor and slipped into Rose's sunporch room. Ellis paused by the windows overlooking the gardens and sea. Soft, mellow late-afternoon light poured into the small room, tinging the walls with gold, and the house was absolutely silent, utterly still. Rose shivered, feeling an eerie sense of timelessness, as if the past thirty years had never passed.

He, too, seemed to sense it, for he walked over to her now in an almost fearful way, and gently, tentatively placed his hands on her, on her shoulders. The way, in the old days, he might approach her for lovemaking. She looked up at him: His face had changed, he had aged, but his eyes were still the same, still pale gray, now hungrily focused on her face: filling, shining. "Rose," he whispered, "I've never forgotten what it was like to be with you." He cupped her face in his hands, and suddenly, there was his mouth again, against hers, his lips parting hers. She had forgotten the amazing mixture of tenderness and passion in his touch, the shape and taste of his mouth, and what it was like to feel this shaky, desperate sort of passion once again.

There was a sharp rap on the door: Startled, she pulled back.

"Mrs. Keating? Are you checking out today? We have to know . . ."

Still in his embrace, she stared up at Ellis, unable to speak for a moment: She wanted only for the embrace never to end, for Ellis never to leave her side again.

"Yes," she said, slowly, haltingly. "I am leaving. I have some . . . important things to do. Some urgent matters to attend to."

"As do I," Ellis replied, in a mournful whisper.

"I don't think," she added, with a rueful laugh, "I could afford another night here." She went to her purse and drew from her wallet a photograph of her daughter. "It's several years old, but it's a good likeness of her."

He gazed at it for a long time. "She looks, I think . . .

like my mother." He placed the photo carefully, tenderly, into his own wallet.

"I wish we had a little more time together."

"I wasn't lying, Rose," he said, suddenly, emphatically, "when I told you years ago that I would forever . . . love you."

She stared at him, her lips parting in surprise.

"I tried to forget you, put you out of my mind, assign you to a dark and distant past. I felt, mistakenly, that to love you was wrong, a clash with my monastic vows. I suppose I was just trying to wall off that pain, that awful ache of having lost you. I know now that I *can* love you—I *must* love, must continue to love you. Loving you means embracing life, embracing God. It's what will keep me alive, and vital, during whatever years are left to me."

"I never stopped, Ellis. Loving you."

He slid his arms around her again, this time in a bracing, comforting way.

"We will have to make do, somehow, with letters. The occasional phone call . . ."

She bit her lip. "You won't be leaving the monastery again?"

"Not for a long while. I was lucky to be granted this leave of absence."

"In a long while . . . you'll be a very old man."

He smiled weakly. "You can come visit me, again. I promise I'll weed my garden, if you'll give me ample warning."

"It's not a trip I could make very often."

He studied her for a long moment, then cupped her face in his hands. In his eyes, she no longer saw the lostness, the emptiness she imagined resided there so many years ago.

"Do you believe in the afterlife, Rose?"

Tears came into her eyes, rolled down her cheeks. "I . . . I don't know. Oh, I want to, Ellis. But—"

"You must believe: You must! Because we will be there, together, one day. I'm sure of it."

✀

In the rearview mirror of her pickup truck, she saw his car following just behind hers as she made her way along country roads to the interstate. Together they crossed the concrete bridge, one behind the other, leaving Wainscott Island forever: They both needed to go south and would travel in the same direction for a while, on a balmy summer's evening, the moon just a slender shining crescent in the sky above. She glanced up often at the mirror, feeling a sweet, splendid comfort just sensing him back there.

But not long after she had maneuvered onto busy I-95 toward Boston, choked now with Sunday-night traffic from the beach crowd, she lost sight of him: He had mingled in with the other cars and had disappeared completely. She felt instantly a wave of sorrow and loss, but tightened her grip on the steering wheel, remembering his words, his embrace. Ellis was still in the world, still in her heart. She could go on.

· A NOTE ON THE TYPE ·

The typeface used in this book is a version of Goudy (Old Style), originally designed by Frederick W. Goudy (1865–1947), perhaps the best known and certainly one of the most prolific of American type designers, who created over a hundred typefaces—the actual number is unknown because a 1939 fire destroyed many of his drawings and "matrices" (molds from which type is cast). Initially a calligrapher, rather than a type cutter or printer, he represented a new breed of designer made possible by late-nineteenth-century technological advance; later on, in order to maintain artistic control, he supervised the production of matrices himself. He was also a tireless promoter of wider awareness of type, with the paradoxical result that the distinctive style of his influential output tends to be associated with his period and, though still a model of taste, can now seem somewhat dated.